"You don't think that I'm scared of you, do you?"

He moved a step closer. "Perhaps you should be," he said softly. A self-mocking gleam lit his eyes. "I'm a little scared of you," he added, to her absolute amazement.

"Of me?" she echoed, in sheer disbelief.

"Why not? When I'm around you, things begin to get a little out of control. And you know how I feel about that."

"You don't like it."

"No, I don't," Nikolaos agreed. He moved still closer. "The problem is, I *do* like *this*."

He took another kiss, longer this time, and more intense.

Dear Reader,

We know from your letters that many of you enjoy traveling to foreign locations—especially from the comfort of your favorite chair. Well, sit back, put your feet up and let Harlequin Presents take you on a yearlong tour of Europe. **Postcards from Europe** will feature a special title every month, set in one of your favorite European countries, written by one of your favorite Harlequin Presents authors. If you're looking for a truly romantic location, come with us to Cyprus— a sunny island that has attracted lovers for centuries. Enjoy your journey.

The Editors

P.S. Don't miss the fascinating facts we've compiled about Cyprus. You'll find them at the end of the story.

HARLEQUIN PRESENTS
Postcards from Europe

JOANNA MANSELL

The Touch of Aphrodite

Harlequin Books

TORONTO • NEW YORK • LONDON
AMSTERDAM • PARIS • SYDNEY • HAMBURG
STOCKHOLM • ATHENS • TOKYO • MILAN
MADRID • WARSAW • BUDAPEST • AUCKLAND

ISBN 0-373-11684-5

THE TOUCH OF APHRODITE

Copyright © 1993 by Joanna Mansell.

This edition published by arrangement with Harlequin Enterprises B. V.

® and TM are trademarks of the publisher. Trademarks indicated with
® are registered in the United States Patent and Trademark Office, the
Canadian Trade Marks Office and other in countries.

Printed in U.S.A.

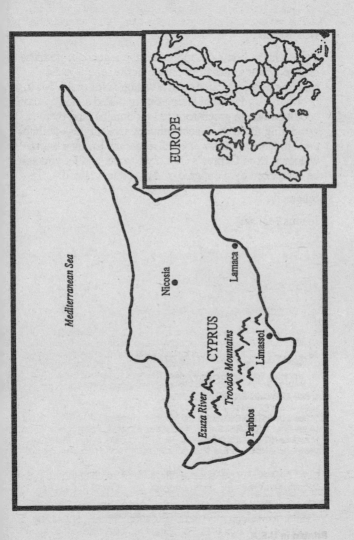

Dear Reader,

Cyprus is the home of Aphrodite, the legendary goddess of love. What writer of romantic fiction could resist weaving a story around such a setting? Not me! Visit it, or simply daydream of lazing on sunbaked sands by day, cooling down in green-forested mountains, and then wandering through ancient ruins by moonlight—perhaps hand in hand with that special someone. Enjoy a warm welcome from Cyprus's friendly people, and let yourself be enchanted by the magic of Aphrodite's island.

Sincerely,

Joanna Mansell

Books by Joanna Mansell

HARLEQUIN PRESENTS

Don't miss any of our special offers. Write to us at the following address for information on our newest releases.

Harlequin Reader Service
U.S.: 3010 Walden Ave., P.O. Box 1325, Buffalo, NY 14269
Canadian: P.O. Box 609, Fort Erie, Ont. L2A 5X3

CHAPTER ONE

EMILY sat bolt upright in her chair and stared in amazement at the solicitor. 'Let's get this straight,' she said in a disbelieving voice. 'My stepfather has left everything — absolutely *everything* — to me? But I can't inherit his estate unless I go and live on Cyprus for a whole year? And, as well as that, I also have to work for my stepfather's nephew, this Nikolaos Konstantin?'

'I'm afraid so,' the solicitor said apologetically. 'The terms of the will are certainly rather unusual, but your stepfather, Dimitri Konstantin, was very specific on this matter.'

On top of all the shocks and upsets of the past few months, it was almost too much to take in. Why had Dimitri wanted to turn her life completely upside-down at the very time when she desperately needed some stability? Emily thought dazedly.

'The whole thing's quite impossible,' she said, with a slow shake of her head. 'My home is here. I can't just sell up and move to a strange country. And what about my job? I'm in the middle of my training as an accountant, I've my next set of exams to take in a few months' time. No,' Emily finished, shaking her head again more firmly, so that her pale gold curls flew out in all directions, 'I simply can't do it. You'll have to find a way around the terms of the will.'

'I'm afraid that's impossible,' the solicitor said politely. 'The will is perfectly valid. Your only chance of breaking it would be if you could prove that your stepfather was mentally incompetent when he made it. Is that a path you would wish to take?'

'No, it certainly isn't,' Emily said, without hesitation. She had adored her stepfather; there was no way she was going to cast any kind of slur on his name. She bit her lip. '*Why* did Dimitri make a will like this?'

'When your stepfather came to me,' said the solicitor in a gentler tone, 'he already knew that he was dying. He told me that his main concern was for you, and what would happen to you after he had gone. He knew that you would be devastated by his death, especially coming so soon after the death of your mother. He believed that it would help you to come to terms with it if you moved right away to a new country, made a fresh start. And Cyprus was the obvious choice, since it was the island of his birth. He also wanted you to meet and be reconciled with the rest of the Konstantin family. I understand that there was a deep rift, following his marriage to your mother?'

'His remarriage to my mother,' Emily said absently. 'And Dimitri's family didn't approve of *either* marriage.' Then, when the solicitor looked surprised, her fair eyebrows lifted. 'Didn't you know? Dimitri and my mother were married when they were very young, but things went wrong, and they split up. Dimitri remained on Cyprus and my mother returned to England. My mother married again, and a couple of years later I was born. My father died when I was ten, though — he worked on the oil rigs, there was an accident. . .' Her voice trailed away for a moment, as a lot of unhappy memories briefly resurfaced. That period of her childhood was a time that she definitely preferred to forget. Then she straightened her shoulders and went on, 'Several years ago, my mother met Dimitri again when he was on a business trip to London. They discovered they were still in love with each other, and remarried.'

'That's a very romantic story,' said the solicitor, with a small smile.

'Except that the happy ending didn't last,' Emily said sadly. 'And now you're telling me that my stepfather has made all these arrangements for me, without even *telling* me?'

'He believed it was for the best,' the solicitor assured her. 'And he did very much want you to be reconciled with his family, since you now have no close relatives of your own.'

'But why do I have to work for his nephew, this Nikolaos Konstantin?' Emily said, puzzled.

'Your stepfather wanted you to gain a better understanding of his business interests. As you probably know, he owned a large five-star hotel on Cyprus. When he came to England to marry your mother, he kept a controlling interest in the hotel, although it was run in his absence by his nephew, Nikolaos. That hotel now forms the major part of your inheritance, and it was your stepfather's wish that you learn how to run it. Nikolaos Konstantin can teach you everything that you need to know.'

'Run the hotel?' Emily repeated, her golden eyebrows shooting up in fresh surprise. She had known, of course, that her stepfather had owned a hotel on Cyprus, and that he had received regular financial reports from his nephew, but she had certainly never expected that Dimitri would want to leave it to her. She wasn't even sure that she wanted it; she didn't know the first thing about running a hotel. Did she want to learn? she asked herself. She didn't know. Right now, the thought of leaving behind everything that was familiar was rather frightening. She felt as if, having lost the two people closest to her, she wanted to cling on to her home, her job, her friends, not go venturing off into the unknown.

'If you live and work on Cyprus for the one year stipulated in the will,' the solicitor went on, 'you'll inherit the hotel, and after that you'll be free to do whatever you want. You can sell up and live off the capital, appoint a manager to run the hotel, or take it over yourself.'

'I really don't think that I could take it over,' she said rather indecisively.

'Of course she can't,' said a male voice dismissively behind her. 'She's just an inexperienced girl. And she isn't even a Konstantin.'

Emily whirled round. Even the solicitor looked briefly startled.

A tall, black-haired man stood just inside the doorway to the office. His dark gaze locked on to Emily's face and then seemed to stay there for an uncomfortable length of time, perhaps longer than he had intended. She found herself holding her breath, and didn't understand why. Except that there was something about this man — his height; the breadth of his shoulders; the dark planes of his face; his sheer *presence* — that would stop most people in their tracks. And his vivid Mediterranean colouring contrasted starkly with the winter pallor of the solicitor's face and Emily's own colourless skin, drained by grief, exhaustion and the shock of so recently losing the two people she had loved most in all the world.

His English was perfect, with only the faintest trace of an accent. Emily realised that she was still staring at him as if hypnotised, and she quickly gathered herself together again.

'Who are you?' she demanded, raw-edged nerves

making her voice sharp. 'And what are you doing here? Were you eavesdropping?'

'I was waiting in the outer office,' the black-haired man said tautly. 'I intended to introduce myself to you later, but in the circumstances I think we should meet right now. I am Nikolaos Konstantin.'

Emily found herself swallowing hard. This was Dimitri's nephew? The man that her stepfather had wanted her to work for? She swallowed again, an almost audible gulp, because even her battered, tired, nervous system had responded to the raw sensuality that glowed in this man's dark eyes, seemed to ooze from his very pores. He was so very *alive*—and definitely in control.

Even the solicitor looked on edge. Nikolaos Konstantin seemed to have that kind of effect on everyone.

'I've just been explaining the conditions of your uncle's will to Miss Peterson——' the solicitor began, in a slightly flustered voice.

'So I heard,' Nikolaos Konstantin cut in. 'The terms of the will are, of course, ridiculous. There is no way that this girl can take over the running of my uncle's hotel.'

His scathing tone of voice made Emily instinctively bristle in response. 'I'm not totally incompetent——' she began.

He didn't even allow her to finish the sentence. 'I can't stop you coming to Cyprus,' he said, those dark eyes boring into her as he looked directly at her, a hot, burning stare that made her pulses suddenly beat jerkily, 'although I would advise against it. I very much doubt if you would be welcomed by any member of the Konstantin family. But I can tell you right now that you are simply too inexperienced to be able to run a top-class hotel. It's a complex business about which you know absolutely nothing. You would simply destroy everything that my uncle spent years building up, and which I have since maintained at the same high standard.'

'I might be inexperienced,' Emily retorted, totally infuriated by his arrogant attitude, 'but that was presumably why Dimitri wanted me to work under you for a while, to *gain* that experience. I am certainly not stupid, and I learn fast.'

He gave a condescending smile, which antagonised her still further. Who did this man think he was? she thought furiously. How dared he walk in here and treat her as if she were a total idiot?

'You must realise that it simply isn't sensible for you even to think of running my uncle's hotel,' he said firmly, as if the matter were already settled.

'I can learn how to do it. I *will* learn how to do it!' Emily declared fiercely, forgetting that, just minutes ago, she had been on the verge of deciding that she didn't even want to go to Cyprus. This man had turned the whole thing into a challenge, though, and a challenge was something that she could rarely resist. Through the grief that had been eating her up lately, she could feel the first stirrings of life, of energy, of the deep need to put just a little of the overwhelming sadness behind her and get on with something positive, something that would help her to get back to a normal life.

Her blue eyes blazed back into Nikolaos's own dark, intense gaze. 'You can't stop me agreeing to the terms of Dimitri's will. All you *can* do is refuse to teach me the things I'll need to know. Are you going to do that?' she demanded, amazed at her own boldness in the face of this man's determined opposition.

Nikolaos Konstantin looked as if he would dearly like to do just that. Eventually, though, he gave a small growl under his breath. 'I promised Dimitri that I would give you every assistance. A promise that is given to a dying man can never be broken.'

'Then that's settled,' Emily said with determination. She turned back to the solicitor. 'I intend to comply with *all* the terms of my stepfather's will. Unless Mr Konstantin has any more objections?' she added, boldly meeting his black gaze again.

Nikolaos looked as if he had plenty of objections. He obviously felt that this was not the right time to voice them, though, and he gave a brief, angry shake of his head. He turned to the solicitor. 'You have the address of my hotel. I'll be there for the next two days. Get in touch with me when you've finalised all the details. I'll then make all the necessary arrangements.'

'Arrangements for what?' Emily asked suspiciously.

'Your trip to Cyprus, of course.'

'Thank you, but I'm perfectly capable of making my own arrangements,' Emily said at once.

'I'm sure that you're capable of a great many things,' he said in a derogatory tone. 'But I agreed to take charge of things after Dimitri's death, and that is exactly what I intend to do.'

Without another word, or even a parting glance at Emily, he then strode out of the room.

Emily stared at the empty doorway for a few seconds, and only realised that her heart had been pounding when it finally began to slow down. Then she at last found her tongue. 'And that's the man that Dimitri arranged for me to work for?' she said incredulously. 'How could he do something like that? There must be other members of his family who could teach me what I need to know!'

The solicitor gave a nervous smile. Nikolaos's presence seemed to have shredded his self-confidence. 'I believe that Mr Nikolaos Konstantin is regarded as the head of the family. He was the obvious choice when your stepfather wanted to make sure that you were left in safe and capable hands.'

'I didn't need to be left in anyone's hands,' Emily said with some determination. Then she shook her head. 'I thought that Dimitri understood me. How could he have done something like this?'

'As I understood it,' said the solicitor, 'your stepfather was very much a Cypriot at heart. And they have a strong tradition of caring for and protecting their women. He simply wanted to uphold those old traditions, and he obviously thought that his nephew was the best man to help you through these next few difficult months.'

Emily was quite certain that Nikolaos Konstantin would simply add to the difficulties that lay ahead of her. And those gleaming black eyes — even just thinking about them sent a deep shiver right through her. She had never seen eyes quite like them before.

'I appreciate that Dimitri was trying to do his best for me. I just wish that he had *consulted* me,' she said at last.

'You don't have to accept the terms of his will,' the solicitor advised her.

'Yes, I do,' she said with a small sigh. 'Dimitri loved me enough to leave me his entire estate and make all these arrangements for my future, even though he was so very ill at the time. I can't just walk away from that. And I loved *him*, so I want to give this a try for his sake.'

The solicitor nodded understandingly. 'Then I'll let Mr Konstantin know that you'll be leaving for Cyprus as soon as all the necessary arrangements have been made.'

As Emily left the solicitor's office and drove back home, she tried to take in the fact that her future had just been turned completely upside-down. She had gone to the solicitor's office expecting to hear that Dimitri had made some kind of financial provision that would let her stay on at the family home for a while, until she had got over the worst of her grief and managed to get her life back on course again. Instead, she had discovered that he had made far-reaching arrangements that were going to cause major disruptions.

Much as she had loved Dimitri, a small part of Emily resented it. Until a few months ago when everything had come to an abrupt halt with, first, her mother's death and then Dimitri's illness, she had been following her own career, she had had a life of her own. Now it seemed that she was going to have to give it all up, at least for the next year. On the other hand, she appreciated that Dimitri had simply tried to do his very best for her, as he had done ever since he had come back into her mother's life nearly seven years ago. Emily had been a rather shy and inexperienced seventeen-year-old then, without a father for all the important formative years of her teens. Although Dimitri had no children of his own, he had seemed to realise at once that Emily, although nearly an adult, still desperately needed a firm but loving father figure in her life. He had been that, and more; a warm man, full of charm, whose dark eyes glowed equally with laughter and passion. A man who had always encouraged her to try new things, take on difficult challenges, attempt the impossible. From the very start, Emily had adored him, and responded to his positive encouragement.

And now in death, as he had done so often in life, he was setting her a new challenge. Forcing her to put aside the awful sadness of the past and face a new future.

Emily lifted her head and blinked away the tears that had begun to glisten in her blue eyes. No more crying. It was time to face the future. She shook back her mane of pale gold hair and told herself that she *would* meet the challenge that Dimitri had set her.

She would go to Cyprus. She would remember both Dimitri and her mother with great love as she tried to rebuild her life without them, and she would make a success of all the things Dimitri wanted her to do. And she would achieve all that with or without the help of Nikolaos Konstantin!

During the next few weeks, Emily often regretted her impulsive decision, but she refused to allow herself to change her mind. And she had to admit to feeling a growing nervous excitement as the time grew near for her to leave England. Or was it the thought of seeing Nikolaos Konstantin again that caused those small shivers to run along her nerve-ends?

Of course not, she told herself staunchly. A lot of women would probably fall for those dark, sensual looks, the glint of danger in those black eyes, but not her!

There was so much to be done before she left that it took her mind off her recent grief, and left her little time to worry endlessly about what lay ahead of her. She contacted an agency about letting the house for the year that she would be away, regretfully gave a month's notice at the firm of accountants where she worked, and began to make lists of all the things she would need to take with her. She said goodbye to her friends, and promised to keep in touch. The house began to look bare as she crated up her personal belongings, ready to be put into storage until she returned. And she was sure that she *would* return. She couldn't imagine herself living in a strange country for the rest of her life.

Nikolaos was arranging all the official paperwork, and sent a message through her solicitor to inform her that he would be in England on business at the end of the month. It would be convenient if she could be ready to travel back with him.

Emily instantly bristled when she got that message. Why should she arrange things for *his* convenience?

When she had calmed down a little, though, she realised that she didn't actually want to travel on her own. The blows of the last few months had knocked a lot of her usual confidence out of her, and she would prefer to make the journey with someone — even Nikolaos Konstantin. Anyway, since they were going to have to work together, it would give them a chance to get to know one another. Perhaps they could get over that poor start and at least be able to be civil to each other.

As the date for her departure grew nearer, Emily found herself fluctuating between a desire to be off, and a deep depression at leaving everything familiar behind. To counteract the depression, she began to go shopping, buying complete new outfits to take with her, finding temporary comfort in the brightness of the shops and the friendly jostle of other people. It wasn't until her credit card statement arrived that she realised just how much she had spent. She was quite appalled at the amount. And she was meant to be training to be an accountant! Too late, she realised what very strange things grief could do to you, how irrationally and irresponsibly it could make you behave. Now she had financial problems to deal with, on top of everything else.

It was almost a relief when, finally, it was time for her to leave. Sleety rain stung Emily's face as she trudged out to the taxi that would take her to the airport. Nikolaos would be waiting there for her. He had already been in England for a couple of days, but there had been just one brief phone call from him in that time, to confirm the arrangements that he had already made through her solicitor. Even so, the sound of his dark velvet voice, with just a hint of an accent, had made her heart thump very much faster than usual.

She had dressed with care, wanting to look mature, efficient and in control. She had chosen a dark, severely cut suit, high-heeled shoes and a thin raincoat that barely kept out the late winter chill. It was a very unsuitable outfit for travelling in, but she didn't care. Dressing so formally gave her confidence, and that was the important thing. Her face was far too pale, but careful make-up helped to disguise it, and a bright lipstick gave her pinched lips much needed colour. And, as a finishing touch, she had drawn back her hair into a sophisticated knot, which completed the look of cool elegance for which she had been striving.

She reached the airport in good time, and Nikolaos was waiting for her in the lounge. Emily gulped hard when she first saw him, standing taller than any of the men around him. She had forgotten — or forced herself to forget — just how *very* impressive he was. The rich tan of his skin was enough to mark him out from the pale faces all around him. And those eyes — so dark, almost black, and piercingly alert. His sheer presence was intimidating and it took all of her courage to walk up to him and give him a cool smile.

His black gaze slid over her, clearly taking in the

sophisticated outfit, the subtly applied make-up. Emily didn't have to be a mind-reader to know what he was thinking—that she didn't look like someone still stricken with grief over the recent loss of her mother and stepfather. More like a fashion model, in fact.

She reminded herself that she didn't care what this man thought of her. She was going to Cyprus to learn how to run a hotel, and Nikolaos Konstantin was going to teach her. That was the extent of her relationship with him.

'It'll be about half an hour before our flight is called,' he said rather curtly. 'Do you want a coffee while you're waiting?'

Emily wasn't sure that her tight throat would actually be able to swallow anything, but she still nodded. It would be better than sitting in awkward silence while they waited for their flight.

In the restaurant, she stared at the cup which was put in front of her, but didn't attempt to touch it. Nikolaos took one mouthful of his own coffee, and then also set it aside.

'At this late stage, I suppose there's no chance of you changing your mind about coming to Cyprus?' he said abruptly.

Emily's head shot up. 'Of course not. All the arrangements have been made.'

A cynical light shone in his eyes. 'And you'd lose your inheritance if you didn't go along with those arrangements, wouldn't you?'

Why was he doing this to her? Emily thought with sudden weariness. Didn't he know what these last few weeks had been like? How difficult it had been to get herself to this stage?

She somehow forced herself to keep her voice even.

'And you think that's all I'm interested in? My inheritance?'

He gave a cool shrug. 'What else?'

'I suppose it hasn't occurred to you that I might be doing this because I loved Dimitri? That I'm simply trying to carry out his wishes?'

'Please keep your voice down,' Nikolaos said evenly, making her realise that, despite all her efforts, her voice had suddenly become shrill with nerves and tension. 'There's no need to make a scene. And no,' he went on, 'I never, for one moment, considered that you were doing this out of any kind of affection for Dimitri. I think that you simply want the good things of life, and the easiest way to get them is with someone else's money.'

Emily couldn't believe that he could accuse her of something so disgusting. She could feel her pale skin going even whiter with rage. 'How *dare* you say something like that to me?' she said furiously. 'Especially since you don't even know me, you've no idea what I'm really like.'

'How dare I?' he said contemptuously. 'Quite easily. And I don't have to know you. I believe you have an old saying in England—like mother, like daughter.'

His words hit her like a physical shock. Then pure fury followed. Her mother had been the least mercenary woman Emily had ever known. Margot Konstantin had been gentle and affectionate, all too easily hurt, and not very good at looking after herself. She certainly hadn't been greedy and grasping, as Nikolaos was implying!

'Are you saying that my mother was only interested in Dimitri because of his money?' she got out in a voice that was still choked with anger.

'Of course. And before you try and deny it, remember that I know all about your mother.'

'What do you know about her?' Emily demanded. 'How *could* you know anything? You never met her.'

'But I know what happened in the past,' Nikolaos said softly, and his black eyes had now begun to glitter dangerously.

The past? What was he talking about? Surely he wasn't going to dredge up all the old antagonism to her mother's original marriage to Dimitri? It had happened such a very long time ago, it was surely time to forgive and forget.

'Are you referring to the first marriage between my mother and Dimitri?' she said in some disbelief. 'But they were just teenagers at the time; they couldn't cope with the problems they ran into and so they split up. All the same, my mother might have coped better if your family had made her feel welcome. But they didn't; right from the very start they made it very clear that they totally disapproved of the marriage.'

'Of course they disapproved,' Nikolaos said in a cold voice. 'Dimitri was already engaged to marry someone else when he met your mother. Just a couple of weeks later, he broke off that engagement and announced his intention of marrying your mother instead.'

'They fell in love,' Emily said defensively. 'They wanted to be together. Surely there was nothing wrong with that?'

She knew at once that she had said the wrong thing. Nikolaos's face became much darker, and the sensual line of his mouth hardened. 'It's certainly wrong to take your own happiness at someone else's expense. The cancelling of that particular engagement caused a great deal of pain and sorrow.'

'I'm sure that Dimitri was very sorry about that. He

was a very caring man; he wouldn't have wanted to upset anyone——'

'*Upset* anyone?' Nikolaos interrupted tersely. 'Two days after he broke off the engagement, his fiancée tried to kill herself. She swam out to sea, and would have kept on going until she drowned, if she hadn't been rescued by a fishing boat.' Ignoring the look of acute shock on Emily's face, he went on bitingly, 'A few months later, she married Dimitri's elder brother. I don't know why she did it—perhaps it was out of revenge, or spite, and just despair. The marriage was a disaster, of course. How could it not be?'

'Look,' said Emily uncomfortably, 'I didn't know any of this. Oh, I knew that my mother and Dimitri had been married before, when they were very young, and that it didn't work out, but that was all. I'm really sorry that it caused so much grief, and I'm beginning to understand why the Konstantin family were so hostile to my mother at the time. But can't you accept that it's all in the past now? It happened over thirty years ago. And when my mother and Dimitri finally met up again they were so happy, they deeply regretted all those years that they spent apart. I think that it really is time that you—that the whole Konstantin family—tried to accept their remarriage, and their love for each other.'

'Love!' Nikolaos said, and there was such cynical contempt in his voice that Emily felt another small wave of shock. 'Love is just an excuse for a man to behave like a fool.'

'I don't think that there was anything in the least foolish about Dimitri,' she retaliated at once.

'He gave up his home and his family, and came to England to remarry your mother, when his first marriage to her had already been a disaster. In my opinion, that was extremely foolish.'

'She made him very happy,' Emily said fiercely.

'Oh, I'm sure that she tried very hard to make him happy,' Nikolaos said scathingly. 'I'm quite certain that she would have done anything to make sure that the Konstantin money didn't slip through her fingers for a second time.'

Emily found his cynicism quite breathtaking. And his attitude completely intolerable. 'That is a *disgusting* thing to say,' she got out in a voice that cracked with renewed anger.

He lifted one hand in a dismissive gesture. 'Spare me all the indignation. I'm not interested. I just wanted to make my own position perfectly clear.'

'You've certainly done that,' she retorted.

'Yet you still intend to come with me to Cyprus?'

'I certainly do,' she said with renewed determination. If this conversation had been aimed at making her change her mind, then he was going to be disappointed! 'I also intend to learn how to run Dimitri's hotel, and at the end of the year claim my full inheritance.'

'That is exactly what I thought you would do,' Nikolaos said coldly. 'And since our flight has just been called I suggest we board the plane.'

They were travelling in the first-class section, which meant that they weren't crammed as close together as they would have been in the tourist section. Even so, Emily felt stifled by Nikolaos's closeness, just inches away in the seat next to hers. She was still blazingly angry at him because of the things he had said, especially about her mother, but at the same time she was uncomfortably aware of his overwhelming maleness; she seemed to feel the heat radiating from that darkly tanned skin, and she didn't have to look at those black eyes to know that they were glowing with repressed energy. She began to feel the first twinges of panic. If he was having this confusing effect on her after only an hour, how on earth was she going to get through the next year?

She stared out of the window, but couldn't see anything except bleak grey clouds. Eventually, she turned back to Nikolaos.

'When we reach Cyprus, where will I live?' she asked rather stiffly.

'I own several hotels,' he said shortly. 'Accommodation won't be a problem.'

'Did Dimitri have a house on the island?'

'He sold all of his personal property when he remarried your mother. It was obvious that he didn't intend to return to Cyprus.'

'Because he knew that his wife wouldn't be made welcome,' Emily retorted.

'Dimitri understood why he had to choose between your mother and his family,' Nikolaos said more harshly.

'Because of all the bad feelings over their first marriage? Well, I think that this silly feud between our two families should come to an end, Mr Konstantin. And you should feel the same. After all, aren't Cypriots meant to value all family ties very highly?'

'Nikolaos,' he said, ignoring what she had just said. 'I think that you should call me Nikolaos.'

'What?' she said, thrown completely off balance by his unexpected response.

His black eyes suddenly glittered again. 'We are, after all, cousins by marriage.'

'Cousins?' she echoed, staring at him in fresh confusion.

'Didn't you know?' His mouth had set into an unnervingly hard line. 'My father is Dimitri's elder brother.'

'But——' Emily abruptly fell silent again as all the implications of his last remark became startlingly clear to her.

'Have you finally worked it out?' Nikolaos said, his eyes fixing on her with an intensity that made her nerves feel quite raw. 'The woman whom Dimitri was engaged to, when he first met your mother—the woman who tried to drown herself when he broke off that engagement—the woman who married Dimitri's elder brother on the rebound—she is my mother.'

Emily tried to swallow, but couldn't, her throat was suddenly too dry.

'I—I didn't know,' she mumbled at last.

'It seems to me that there's a great deal you don't know,' Nikolaos said softly. 'You're either very ignorant, or simply not interested in the history of your family.'

That remark stung because there was an element of truth in it. Emily had been so relieved when her mother's remarriage to Dimitri had worked out so marvellously that she had determined to put all the unhappy past behind her. She had decided not to ask any questions which would stir up bad memories or cast a shadow on their happiness. She was beginning to regret that now, because she found herself uneasily wondering just what else she had to learn about the Konstantin family.

For much of the rest of the flight, she tried to read a book, but it was hard—in fact, almost impossible—to concentrate on the words. She was too aware of Nikolaos sitting beside her, engrossed in some paperwork now, but still radiating that powerful presence which she found so very disturbing.

Eventually, he raised his head, glanced out of the window, and then seemed to relax a fraction.

'We're nearly home,' he said, with some satisfaction.

Emily was about to say that it was his home, not hers, but the words slipped out of her head and were forgotten as she looked out of the window. The grey clouds had disappeared, the sun was shining hazily down out of a pale azure sky on to a soft blue sea, and the island of Cyprus rose out of the gently lapping water, coloured gold and green by the winter sunshine.

'The island of love,' Nikolaos murmured as he saw the rapt look on her face, and a note of cynicism was back in his voice now.

Emily ignored it. She was entranced by her first sight of the island. 'It's also the home of Aphrodite, the goddess of love and beauty,' she added softly, remembering the stories from the books she had read during the past few weeks. 'She rose from the foam of the sea and bewitched men, filled them with sweet desire.' Then she realised that her skin felt suddenly hot, and her nerve-ends were tingling in a strange way.

'That is only a legend,' Nikolaos pointed out.

'Of course it is,' she agreed quickly, flushing hard and wondering what on earth had made her say something like that. And to Nikolaos, of all people!

She reminded herself that it definitely wouldn't be a good idea to let herself be bewitched by this island; she was here to learn how to run a hotel, and claim her inheritance, that was all. All the same, her gaze became a little dreamy as she saw the blue seas and the green forests, the beaches that glowed in the sun and the patches of colour from early spring flowers.

As the plane neared Larnaca airport, it flew over a wide lake with pink clouds floating on its surface. Emily frowned in puzzlement. Pink clouds? Clouds that floated on water? Then she realised what she was looking at.

'Flamingos!' she exclaimed out loud. 'Whole flocks of flamingos.'

Nikolaos looked at her consideringly, as if he hadn't expected her to be so obviously delighted with her first glimpses of the island.

'That's a salt lake,' he told her, after a short pause. 'The birds spend the winter there, and in the summer, when the lake dries up, the salt is collected.'

The plane began its approach towards the runway, and Emily twisted a few stray strands of hair back into the golden knot at the nape of her neck. She knew that it was silly, it really didn't matter what she looked like. There wasn't going to be a whole crowd of Konstantins waiting for her at the airport, to welcome her. She didn't know one single person on this island—except for Nikolaos.

She took a quick look at his dark face, shuttered again now, as if to deliberately keep her out of his private thoughts. Then the plane wheels gently bumped against the runway and suddenly it didn't matter, she was here on Cyprus, and she knew that she was *glad* that she was here. Glad that she had had the courage to tackle this new challenge. And she wasn't going to let Nikolaos Konstantin be a problem. She was going to get through the next year without any more pain, any more sadness, any more emotional turmoil.

Over the past few months, her life had hit rock-bottom. Now she was sure that it was slowly on the way up again.

CHAPTER TWO

AFTER the plane had landed, Nikolaos whizzed her through all the formalities with astonishing speed. Then he collected her luggage.

'The excess charge on this is sky-high,' he said rather grimly.

Emily looked edgily at the great pile of suitcases and hoped there was no way he could find out that they were stuffed with all the clothes she had bought on that reckless spending spree. She hadn't been able to find enough energy to return them to the shops, and had felt too guilty to leave them behind.

'I am staying for a whole year,' she said defensively.

'We do have shops here, on Cyprus,' Nikolaos pointed out. 'You could have packed just a few essential things, and bought everything else you needed once you were here.' Then his mouth set into a cynical line. 'But I suppose that you enjoyed spending Dimitri's money. Does everything in those suitcases have an expensive designer label on it?'

'I didn't spend a penny that wasn't my own,' Emily retorted, fiercely resenting his implication that she couldn't wait to rush out and spend some of her stepfather's money. 'I haven't been living on Dimitri's charity for the past few years.'

Nikolaos looked sceptical, but didn't press the point any further. 'Follow me to the car,' he said instead, in a crisp tone.

'Our bags ——' began Emily.

'The chauffeur will bring them.' He signalled to a

broad-shouldered man standing near by, whom Emily hadn't noticed until now. Then he walked quickly towards the exit, leaving Emily to hurry after him.

The car that was waiting outside was dark, sleek and powerful. Like its owner, Emily muttered to herself, as she sank into the soft leather seat in the back. Then her nerves gave a hefty twitch as Nikolaos got in beside her. Edgily, she began to wonder if she was *always* going to react like this every time he came close to her.

'You'll be staying in my hotel in Larnaca,' he told her, as the car moved smoothly away. 'You'll obviously need a few days to settle in—and unpack,' he added caustically, with obvious reference to the amount of luggage she had brought with her. 'We'll wait until next week before getting down to any serious work.'

'Why do I have to stay in your hotel?' Emily asked, knowing that she would feel a lot more relaxed if she could keep some distance between herself and this disturbingly attractive man.

'Because I promised Dimitri that I would look after you.'

'I don't need looking after,' she insisted at once. 'Especially since you're only doing it out of a sense of duty. You really don't want me here at all, do you, Mr Konstantin?'

'Nikolaos,' he corrected her softly. 'I told you to call me Nikolaos.'

But Emily didn't want to be reminded of the fact that they were cousins, even if cousins only by marriage, with no actual blood ties between them. She sat in tense silence for the rest of the journey, and was relieved when the car finally drew up outside a hotel which was situated right on the promenade, and overlooking the marina.

Nikolaos took her straight up to what was obviously

one of the best rooms in the hotel. It had a balcony overlooking the sea, and the sun shone in gently through the wide windows.

'This is very nice,' Emily said, forcing herself to be polite. 'But, of course, I can only stay here for a couple of nights, at the most.'

Nikolaos's gaze narrowed. 'Why?'

'Because I need a place of my own. I can't spend the next twelve months living in hotels. Perhaps I could find a small apartment ——'

'And how would you pay for it?' he enquired coolly. 'You won't inherit the bulk of Dimitri's estate until your year here is up. And I doubt if you've very much money left of your own, if the amount of luggage you've brought with you is a reliable indication of your spending habits.'

Emily flushed because, of course, he was right. Why, oh *why* had she gone on that wild shopping spree? It had virtually wiped out her savings, leaving her financially vulnerable. And *any* kind of vulnerability had to be dangerous where this man was concerned.

'I'll be earning a salary while I'm learning the hotel business,' she said with renewed stubbornness, determined to fight for her independence. 'I can pay for some kind of accommodation out of that.'

For just an instant, Nikolaos looked surprised, as if he had expected her to welcome the chance to live in his hotel free of charge. Then he waved his hand dismissively. 'It's far more practical for you to live in the hotel. Once you begin your training, you'll be working at all hours of the day and night because the hotel trade is a twenty-four-hour-a-day business. It wouldn't make sense for you to live some distance away.'

'I thought that you didn't even want me working

under you, let alone living under your roof,' she pointed out. 'In fact, considering the way that you feel about me, I don't know why you've taken any of this on at all. Surely it would have been better to let someone else handle this whole thing?'

'I couldn't do that,' Nikolaos said in a rather grim tone. 'I gave my word to my uncle that I would handle this myself, and I have to keep that word. I don't approve of the will that Dimitri made, nor do I think that you have any right to his estate, but I will still do everything I can to carry out his last wishes.'

Well, that was plain enough! Emily told herself. Nikolaos Konstantin had made it absolutely clear that any help he gave her would be purely out of a sense of duty.

'I'll speak to you again in the morning,' he went on in a more controlled voice. 'If you want something to eat, the hotel restaurant is open at the usual hours.'

After he had gone, a couple of bellboys staggered in with her luggage, and she became embarrassed all over again as she realised just how much she had brought with her. She unpacked a couple of cases, and winced as she remembered just how much all these new clothes had cost.

A little later, she went down and ordered dinner in the hotel restaurant, feeling rather self-conscious sitting at a table all by herself. At the end of her meal, though, when she tried to pay the bill, she discovered that Nikolaos had left instructions that all her expenses would be taken care of by him. Emily was used to paying her own way, so that was something that would definitely have to change. In the morning, she would make that very clear to Nikolaos.

For tonight, though, she simply wanted to sleep. It had been a long and emotionally exhausting day, and

the couple of glasses of local wine that she had had
with her dinner were now adding to her drowsiness.
She went back to her room, crawled between the crisp,
cool sheets and immediately fell asleep.

In the morning, she woke up to find that the sun was
again shining palely down out of a clear blue sky. She
had read that Cyprus in February could sometimes be
chilly and wet, but this was obviously going to be a
golden, sun-filled day, a welcome change from the grey
weather she had left behind in England.

Emily quickly showered and dressed. She decided
against breakfast, because she didn't want to eat
another thing in this hotel until she had sorted out the
question of payment for her food with Nikolaos.
Instead, she left the hotel and headed for the promenade, which was long and lined with tall palm trees,
reminding her of the south of France.

She strolled down towards the marina, where lines
of yachts bobbed quietly, some quite small, others
white and gleaming and expensive. Even this early
there were quite a few other people around, some of
them heading for the beach although it really wasn't
warm enough yet for sunbathing. Quite a few of them
smiled at Emily as they passed her, and she found
herself smiling back. People here seemed different
from back home. More friendly, more relaxed. Of
course, a lot of them were obviously on holiday, which
made a difference. But there was something welcoming
about the atmosphere; people were calling out to each
other and joking as they opened up the shops that lined
the promenade; they were obviously happy in their
work and looking forward to the day ahead. It was very
different from the big city rush that Emily was used to,
with everyone grimly jostling for space on overcrowded
Tubes and buses, or hurrying along with heads down,

ignoring the people around them, intent only on getting to work on time.

Then Emily gave a small gulp as she suddenly saw a face that was very familiar. Nikolaos, walking purposefully in her direction, dressed very formally today in a dark suit and crisp white shirt, and looking more imposing than ever.

Emily gave a silent groan. What was he doing here? Was he looking for her? As he drew nearer, though, his dark gaze fixed on her, and she realised that he looked rather surprised to see her. So, this meeting was purely coincidental.

As he drew level with her, his black brows set into a distinct frown, as if he wasn't particularly pleased to see her.

'You're up early,' he said shortly.

'What did you expect?' she replied. 'That I would lie in bed half the morning? I'm not a lazy person!'

'I thought that, after the long journey yesterday, you might have relaxed and ordered breakfast in bed,' Nikolaos said after a brief pause.

That immediately reminded Emily of something that she needed to get settled right now.

'I'm not ordering anything in your hotel until we've sorted out the question of the bill,' she said at once.

Nikolaos's frown deepened. 'It's already been taken care of. All your expenses will be met by the hotel.'

'They certainly will not,' she retorted. 'I'm used to paying my own way. I won't be treated like some — some charity case!'

'What is this?' Nikolaos said cynically. 'Some ploy to impress me? A way of trying to convince me that you're independent, and don't accept other people's money?'

Emily felt a huge rush of frustration. What did she

have to do to get through to this man? Convince him that she wasn't interested in free rides?

'I'm not the kind of person who wants something for nothing,' she said hotly.

'Then why are you accepting the inheritance that Dimitri left you?' he countered immediately.

'That's — that's different.'

'In what way?' he enquired coolly.

'In *every* way,' she told him angrily. 'And you know it!'

His face immediately hardened. 'All I know is that I am under an obligation to provide you with everything that you need during the coming year. And if you want to comply with the terms of Dimitri's will, then you are obliged to accept that fact. And my guess is that you will accept it,' he added in a harsher voice. 'Nothing is going to stop you from claiming Dimitri's estate, is it?'

Emily gave a sudden, deep sigh and abandoned the argument. She was quite sure that she couldn't say or do anything to change this man's opinion of her. He had labelled her a fortune hunter, and that was how she would forever remain in his eyes. Anyway, it didn't *matter*, she told herself defiantly. She was here to learn how to run Dimitri's hotel; nothing else was really important.

She turned round and began to walk away from Nikolaos, towards the marina. Then she was rather disconcerted to find that he had begun to stride along beside her.

'Why are you following me?' she demanded. 'You don't have to keep a watch over me, I'm not going to do anything that will disgrace the Konstantin family!'

'I'm not following you,' he said curtly. 'I'm on my way to the marina. Some friends of mine are using my yacht today. I've a business meeting shortly, but before

I leave I want to check that everything's ready for them.'

'Your yacht?' Emily echoed. Her gaze skimmed over the lines of boats lying at anchor. 'Which one is it? No, let me guess,' she went on with a touch of sarcasm. 'The biggest and most expensive!'

His dark eyes fixed on her scathingly. 'Do you think that I need to flaunt my wealth?' Then he walked on towards the marina, and agilely jumped aboard a medium-sized yacht moored near the jetty.

Emily gave a small sigh. She just didn't seem to be able to say the right thing to Nikolaos. And this was the man she had to work with for the next year!

Of course, it was all his fault, she told herself staunchly. He was so hostile and arrogant. But the whole situation was going to become quite impossible if they continued like this for the next twelve months. In fact, she really didn't think she could cope with it. She was so completely on her own, with not even a friend she could talk things over with. Some sort of compromise had to be reached, or she was never going to make it through the year; she would panic, crumble, or just give up and run for home.

They needed to talk, she decided. And right now, before her courage failed her.

She sat down on a bench near the marina and waited for Nikolaos to return from his yacht. She discovered that her heart was thumping rather fast and firmly told herself that was silly, there was absolutely no reason why she should be nervous of Nikolaos. Yet that didn't stop her skin from prickling in a most peculiar way when she finally saw him leaving the marina again.

When Nikolaos saw her sitting there, waiting for him, he stopped dead and the dark frown reappeared on his face.

'I don't have the time — or the inclination — to talk with you any further today,' he said tersely.

His deliberate brusqueness very nearly made Emily get up and walk off. Instead, though, she forced herself to stay exactly where she was. She knew that she was the one who would have to make the first gesture — although it would probably be the hardest thing that she would ever do!

'I think that perhaps I should apologise,' she said at last, forcing out the words because she really didn't think she had done anything that she needed to apologise for; she was simply trying to soften his attitude towards her.

Instead of responding sympathetically, a look of extreme scepticism immediately appeared on Nikolaos's face. 'Do I detect a certain lack of sincerity in your voice?' he drawled.

Emily was alarmed that he had picked that up so easily. What else had she revealed just by the tone of her voice?

'I — er — I —— ' she began, totally flustered. Then she managed to get control of herself again. 'I'm simply trying to do something about this impossible situation,' she went on much more steadily. 'I want to end all this antagonism between us.'

Nikolaos glanced at his watch. 'This conversation will have to wait,' he said curtly. 'I'm already late for my business appointment.'

Emily knew that if she gave up now, though, she might not find enough nerve to tackle this subject again. 'Let me walk with you,' she suggested. 'I really do want to talk to you.'

'I'm not walking, I'm driving — to Nicosia. If you want to discuss something, you'll have to come with me.'

'To Nicosia?' she said, blinking.

'It's only fifty kilometres,' he pointed out, with a touch of impatience. 'I'm not suggesting that you come with me to the end of the world.'

'But — what would I do when I get there?'

'That really isn't my concern.'

'I suppose I could go sightseeing,' she said, after a moment's thought. 'How long will your business meeting take?'

'A couple of hours.'

'And I could return with you afterwards, to Larnaca?'

'I wasn't proposing to leave you stranded in Nicosia,' he said drily.

'Then I'll come,' she told him. She really did want to talk to him and try to get something sorted out today, while her nerve was still holding and she could stand up to this man.

His car was waiting for him in front of the hotel. Nikolaos opened the passenger door for Emily, and then slid into the front seat beside her.

'No chauffeur today?' she asked.

'I only use him on formal occasions.'

'Our trip from the airport to the hotel was hardly a formal affair,' she pointed out.

'But, in a way, it was, since it marked your arrival on Cyprus. Whether I like it or not, you are, at least temporarily, part of the Konstantin family. That means that you have to be treated with a certain amount of respect.'

'Even though it sticks in your throat,' Emily said caustically.

Nikolaos merely shrugged. 'Given the conditions of Dimitri's will, it was inevitable that you would come to

Cyprus. It doesn't have to be inevitable that you stay, though.'

She immediately looked at him suspiciously. 'What do you mean?'

'That there's no reason why we shouldn't come to some kind of—arrangement.'

'What sort of arrangement?' Emily asked at once. At the same time, her pale gold brows drew together. She had agreed to come on this trip because she had wanted to discuss certain things with him, and also try—although she had very little hope of success—to put right the very biased opinion he had of her. She had hoped to be able to make him see that life would be much easier for both of them if they could make an effort to start again, forget about their past differences and try to forge some kind of working relationship that would get them through the next few months. It rather looked as if Nikolaos Konstantin had very different ideas, however!

'You intend to claim Dimitri's estate,' he now said in a very cool voice. 'I happen to think that you shouldn't have it. It belongs to his family.'

'I *am* his family,' Emily said indignantly. 'My mother was his wife!'

'For only a few years,' Nikolaos pointed out. 'And you are only his stepdaughter. As far as I'm concerned, that gives you no rights at all. You aren't a blood relative, you don't even use the name of Konstantin. You keep the name of your own father, Peterson. Although, as it happens, that's the one thing that I do approve of. You have no right to be known as Emily Konstantin.'

'You keep talking of rights,' Emily retorted furiously, 'but it seems to me that you want to deny them to Dimitri, your uncle. He was entitled to do hatever he liked with his estate, and he made his ishes perfectly clear. He wanted to leave it to *me*. ou won't accept that, though, you keep trying to verride his wishes.'

'Marriage to your mother made Dimitri forget that e had other obligations,' Nikolaos said in a much arsher tone. 'He has three elderly aunts, another ephew and two nieces. There is also myself, of course, lthough I am certainly not interested in claiming any art of his estate for myself. But my family are his lood relations, and therefore they are entitled to at ast part of any interitance.'

Emily was a little shaken by this statement, because le had never considered the fact that Dimitri might ave members of his own family who might benefit om a part of his estate.

'Are you saying that these aunts, his nephew and ieces, are in need of money?' she said hesitantly. 'That ley will be in real hardship if they don't get it?'

'Of course not,' Nikolaos said dismissively. 'They are ll Konstantins; no member of the family would be llowed to fall into financial hardship. I would see to lat.'

'Then what is this all about?' Emily said a little more ndignantly.

'I am telling you that they have a more rightful claim o his estate than you do.'

'Are they going to *make* a claim on it?'

'No,' he said, after a short pause.

'Then it's just you who's stirring up all this trouble, n't it?' she said angrily. 'You want *them* to have it, nstead of me. In fact, you don't really care who gets , as long as it isn't me!'

Nikolaos's face became even more grim. 'It's bviously impossible to talk to you about this,' he said tersely. 'You don't seem to have any sense of decenc or honour. You are simply a fortune hunter, like yo mother.'

That made Emily completely lose her temper. H could say what he liked about her, but he was *not* goin to denigrate her mother!

'Dimitri was very happy with my mother,' she said i an outraged tone. 'He loved her; in fact, he adore her! All he wanted was to be with her.'

'My uncle was obsessed,' Nikolaos said dismissively 'He gave up his home, his family, everything, just t satisfy his desire for your mother.'

'He wasn't obsessed. He was in love!' Emily glare at him fiercely. 'Can't you understand that? Don't yo know what love is, what it's like?'

'I certainly understand desire, and the madness it ca cause. But marriage should be based on more tha that; it should include respect and affection and per manent commitment.'

'Dimitri's marriage to my mother included all o those things. If you'd seen them together, you'd hav known that. Are you married?' she demanded.

'No,' he said rather curtly.

'Well, I'm not surprised, considering your cynica attitude towards other people's marriages,' sh retorted. 'I hope, for the sake of the women of Cyprus that you stay single all your life!'

'One day, I will want a family. Then I will marry,' h said tersely. 'But I will be very careful of my choice o partner. Make the wrong choice and too many peopl can be affected by the far-reaching consequences. I my uncle's case, because of his obsessional love fo your mother, his family have been deprived of thei rightful inheritance, and I have to spend a year of m life looking after a woman who means nothing to me.'

His last words hurt far more than he had probably intended. Emily was alarmed at just how much they stung, and retaliated fiercely to try and cover up her reaction. 'You do *not* have to look after me. I'm not stupid or helpless, I'm perfectly capable of looking after myself. And you seem to be forgetting that this arrangement has disrupted *my* life, as well as yours. Unlike you, though, I'm trying to make the best of it. That's why I wanted to talk to you today, to see if we could put an end to all this hostility. That's obviously going to be quite impossible, though. You're clearly not interested in calling some kind of truce, or trying to make things easier and more pleasant for both of us.'

'I'm certainly not interested in making *your* life easy or pleasant,' Nikolaos said brutally. 'On the other hand, I can see that you've got a great incentive for wanting to get through the next few months with the minimum of trouble. After all, at the end of it, you're going to get your inheritance. And that's all you're really interested in, isn't it?'

'Oh, I give up,' Emily said in sudden despair. 'Trying to talk to you is just impossible. You've got such fixed, biased ideas about me, and they're never going to change, are they?'

'No,' he said flatly, then he put his foot down hard on the accelerator and sent the car hurtling along the motorway.

They drove on to Nicosia in absolute silence. Emily wished that she had never set foot in this car, had never been stupid enough to think that she could reason with Nikolaos Konstantin, and couldn't wait for this trip to be over.

When they finally reached Nicosia, Emily asked in a tight voice to be dropped outside the Cyprus museum.

'Do you intend to improve your mind?' Nikolaos enquired caustically.

'I'm well aware that you don't think I've got a mind to improve,' she retorted.

'To the contrary,' he replied softly. 'I think that you've got a very clever, and probably devious mind.'

'You also think that I'm greedy, unscrupulous and unprincipled,' Emily said accusingly.

'Your words, not mine,' he reminded her. He glanced at his watch. 'I'll pick you up in two hours.' Then, as soon as Emily had got out of the car, he swiftly drove off.

By that time, Emily wasn't exactly in the right frame of mind to appreciate the ancient culture of Cyprus. She couldn't just wander around aimlessly for the next couple of hours, though, so she trudged through the porticoed entrance of the museum.

As she wandered slowly through the rooms, staring at terracotta figures of warriors, charioteers and mythical minotaurs, statues in stone, bronze and marble, helmets and weapons, drinking cups, necklaces, and a cauldron decorated with griffins and double-faced sirens, she soon became absorbed in what she was seeing. Here was Cyprus's fascinating, turbulent and often blood-stained history, stretching right back to Neolithic times. The island had been ruled by the Romans, invaded by the Saracens, conquered by Richard the Lionheart. Phoenician traders had beached their galleys on the golden sands, Venetian merchants had sold their goods in the streets of Nicosia, the Knights of St John administered great estates that produced sugar cane and the famous Cyprus wine.

Emily stood for the longest amount of time, however, in front of the marble statue of Aphrodite. Here she was, the legendary goddess of love who had made her home on Cyprus, the temptress of all men, unfaithful to her husband, flitting from lover to lover. And yet, according to legend, when one of her lovers, Adonis, was killed by another of her lovers disguised as a boar, the inconsolable Aphrodite had wept, and from her tears had sprung the red and white anemones that now covered the island.

Emily gave a rueful smile. What would it be like to have such a tempestuous love life? She had absolutely no idea. She had had a couple of semi-serious relationships, but she had never been in love. Sometimes, she thought that she never would be. Part of her shied away from it; she knew — like Nikolaos — that love could have its darker side.

Her mother's second marriage, to Emily's father, had been very unhappy, and as a child Emily had seen far too much of the damage that could result when love turned sour. She had even experienced some of that damage herself, when her father's anger and frustration had boiled over into a violence that had lashed out indiscriminately in all directions. She gave a small shudder as old, painful memories briefly surfaced. Then she pushed them away again, locked them away in the very back of her mind, where they couldn't hurt her. She rarely thought of those dark times nowadays. Dimitri's generous affection, compassion and surprising gentleness had helped to heal a lot of the old wounds. And the happiness he had obviously found in marriage to her mother had helped to convince Emily that a relationship could work marvellously well when love was deep and mutual.

She reluctantly walked away from the statue of the fascinating Aphrodite, left the museum, crossed the road and went into the Municipal Gardens. She found a seat shaded by palm trees, and sat down to wait for Nikolaos to return.

She certainly wasn't looking forward to the return trip to Larnaca. The only good thing was that, at the speed Nikolaos drove, it wouldn't take too long. Fortunately, he was an excellent driver, handling the large, powerful car with effortless skill.

Nikolaos drew up outside the museum half an hour later, exactly on time. Emily walked towards the car, but then slowed down when she saw that he wasn't alone.

A woman, perhaps a couple of years older than Emily, sat beside him. She had very dark hair that fell in luxuriant waves to her shoulders, and eyes that were almost black. Her face was nearly, but not quite beautiful, with strong bones and a full mouth, and she had the same aura of dark sensuality that radiated from Nikolaos, although it was more subtle and feminine.

As Emily climbed into the back seat, she noted the other woman's air of confidence and sophistication, and immediately felt at a disadvantage. She knew that she couldn't match it, at least not at the moment. Too much had happened over the past few months; the strain of coping with everything had knocked a lot of her own self-assurance out of her, although she still managed to put on a brave show when circumstances demanded it. Underneath, though, her nerves all too often felt completely ragged, and it was hard to be the capable, confident Emily that she had once been.

As Nikolaos drove away, however, and the woman beside him turned to look at her, Emily managed to produce a friendly smile.

'I'm Emily Peterson——' she introduced herself.

'This is Sofia,' Nikolaos cut in. 'She's a cousin of mine.'

Emily's heart immediately sank. If this woman was another Konstantin, then she couldn't expect a very warm response.

She was right. Sofia didn't give Emily an answering smile. Instead, her dark gaze ran swiftly over her, scrutinising her with some intensity. 'Nikolaos and I have known each other for most of our lives,' she said at last, in a low and rather husky tone. 'We are very close friends, as well as cousins.' She obviously didn't intend that Emily should miss the implication of that remark, and looked at Emily's face carefully, to make sure that she had got the message. Emily tried hard to keep her expression completely neutral, but wasn't completely sure that she had succeeded.

In a very cool voice, Sofia went on, 'I know who you are, of course. I have heard about you from my family.'

Her English was as good as Nikolaos's. There was nothing in the least friendly in her tone of voice, though. Emily gave a silent sigh. She supposed that Sofia knew all about Dimitri's will and, like Nikolaos, intensely disapproved of the way he had left his estate.

She sighed again, more audibly this time. The next few months were going to be very difficult if the entire Konstantin family were against her. She had to make a real effort to win at least some of them over to her side, Emily told herself. It was obviously no use attempting it with Nikolaos; his opinion of her was absolutely entrenched, and there didn't seem to be anything on this earth she could say or do to change it. But Sofia was a woman, and near to her own age. They might even find that they had a lot in common, if they could just get past this initial hostility.

Emily tried another friendly smile, which got no response at all. She didn't give up, though. Instead, she asked in a warm voice, 'Do you live in Nicosia?'

'My family owns an apartment there,' Sofia said distantly. 'We also have a house in Limassol, and another in the Troodos mountains.'

Emily was beginning to realise that the Konstantin family was far more wealthy and influential than she had realised. Before coming to Cyprus, she had rather naïvely assumed that Dimitri had been the success story in the family; the one who has raised his prestigious hotel to five-star status. She had obviously been wrong about that, though. From the little she had learnt, Nikolaos's business interests seemed to be widespread and varied, and obviously highly lucrative. But if the family had so much money, why were they making all this fuss about Dimitri's estate being left to *her*? Emily wondered with a puzzled frown.

'Are you really going to work for Nikolaos for the next few months?' Sofia asked abruptly, interrupting Emily's thoughts.

Emily shrugged. 'I don't have much choice. It's a condition of Dimitri's will.'

'Dimitri's will!' Sofia repeated, with obvious impatience. 'I don't understand why it should be causing all these problems. Surely you can break the will, Nikolaos?'

He turned his head and gave her an unexpectedly indulgent look, as if he was well used to her impatience. 'If it were up to me, I could and I would. But the rest of Dimitri's family won't agree.'

'Can't you talk to them?'

'I already have. Their decision was firm and final, though, and I won't try again to change their minds. They have the right to do as they think best.'

'Then it's up to *you* to do something,' Sofia declared, turning back to Emily. 'You know that the will isn't right or fair; you must tell your solicitor that you won't accept its terms.'

But Emily was getting rather tired of the Konstantin family telling her what she should or shouldn't do. Also, she was discovering that she didn't like Sofia very much. There was something hard and self-centred in her eyes and mouth, a spoilt wilfulness in her tone of voice. Emily was already abandoning any plans she might have had to try and befriend her.

'I don't intend to go against Dimitri's wishes,' she said steadily.

'Nikolaos, *please* do something about this,' Sofia said pleadingly, a soft, husky undertone to her voice. 'You must make her give up this claim.'

But Emily had had more than enough of this particular conversation. 'Dimitri's will was very clear, and there are no grounds on which anyone could contend it,' she declared very firmly. 'And if you give me any more trouble about it, then I might have to take legal steps to prevent it.'

Too late, she realised that sounded like a threat. And Emily knew instinctively that no one in their right mind would ever issue a threat against Nikolaos Konstantin. Even Sofia looked startled, as if she had never heard anyone do anything quite so rash before.

Nikolaos raised his gaze briefly to the driving mirror, so that he could look directly at Emily. She shivered slightly under that dark, angry scrutiny, but then reminded herself that he couldn't actually *do* anything. Not while he was driving, and also had his cousin sitting beside him.

His voice when he next spoke, though, reminded her that there were more ways than one of inflicting damage.

'If you take any kind of legal action against me, I

promise you that you will be very sorry,' he said with soft menace.

Emily didn't say another word, and even Sofia seemed subdued by Nikoloas's grim tone. The car sped on to Larnaca, through the low, rounded hills covered with fresh spring greenery and tiny splashes of colour from early flowers. But not another word was spoken by the three people in the car during the entire journey.

CHAPTER THREE

WHEN they finally reached Larnaca, instead of taking Emily straight back to the hotel, Nikolaos instead brought the car to a halt outside a large office building.

'I have to see someone about a business matter,' he said briefly. 'It will only take a few minutes. If you don't mind waiting, Emily, I'll take you to the hotel directly afterwards.'

'No, I don't mind,' she said with resignation. The journey from Nicosia had already seemed quite interminable. It wouldn't matter if it dragged on for a while longer.

After he had gone into the building, an uncomfortable silence filled the car. Sofia sat with her elegant head slightly turned away and made no effort to speak, so it was Emily who finally broke the silence.

'Did you meet Nikolaos in Nicosia by chance?' she asked.

'Of course not,' Sofia replied in a frosty tone. 'The meeting was arranged several days ago. Nikolaos and I have some family business to attend to here, in Larnaca, and then we are having dinner together tonight.'

'Oh,' said Emily, and she found herself swallowing rather harder than she intended. She was alarmed to discover that she didn't like the idea of Sofia and Nikolaos sharing what would probably be an intimate meal. That was ridiculous, of course, because it was absolutely none of her business. She hurriedly told herself that she really didn't *care* that Nikolaos and Sofia had a dinner date.

'I—I expect that you see quite a lot of Nikolaos?' Emily forced herself to say.

Sofia's dark eyes suddenly glittered with hostility. 'Yes. But you'll be seeing far more of him during the next few months.'

Emily got the message at once. She also decided that this was one misunderstanding that she could put right straight away. She didn't like Sofia very much, and the feeling was obviously mutual, but there was no need for there to be animosity between them because of Nikolaos, and she intended to make that perfectly clear.

'Look, let's get one thing straight,' she said in a very firm voice. 'Nikolaos and I will be working together— and that is all.'

'Please don't make the mistake of thinking that I'm naïve,' Sofia said, in a brittle tone.

Emily thought that naïve was just about the very last word she would ever have used to describe the sophisticated, worldly Sofia. She was determined to get this sorted out, though, before Nikolaos came back.

'I'm here on Cyprus to learn about Dimitri's business affairs,' she said evenly. 'Nikolaos doesn't want me here, but because of the terms of Dimitri's will he has to spend the next year trying to teach me the things I'll need to know. It's not an ideal situation, but we're both adults and I'm sure that we can cope with it.' Privately, Emily had deep reservations about her ability to cope with Nikolaos, but she certainly wasn't going to admit that to Sofia.

But Sofia was already staring at her with renewed hostility. 'And why do you suppose that Dimitri wrote that ridiculous proviso into his will?' she said, her dark eyes flashing.

'I'd have thought that was obvious——' Emily began.

'Of course it's obvious!' Sofia interrupted angrily. 'Dimitri was always a stupid romantic. Even a child could realise what he had in mind, forcing you, his adored stepdaughter, and Nikolaos, his favourite nephew, to work together and spend so much time in each other's company!'

Emily blinked in genuine astonishment as she realised what Sofia was implying. Was *she* the one who had been naïve? Was that really what Dimitri had had in mind? She remembered how he had sometimes gently teased her over the fact that she was nearly twenty-four and still not married. She knew that he had wanted to see her with a husband and children, and had always looked concerned when she had told him that she was a career girl at heart. But surely he wouldn't go so far as to try and manipulate her into a relationship?

'No, you're wrong,' she said finally, with a quick shake of her head. 'Dimitri would never do anything like that.'

'Of course he would,' Sofia said scornfully. 'In his mind, it would have been the perfect solution. You don't really think that he intended that someone like *you* should run his hotel, do you? He wanted to bring you and Nikolaos together, so that you would be safely married, and Nikolaos, as your husband, would keep control of Dimitri's business concerns.'

Marriage to Nikolaos—for just a few dazzling moments, Emily allowed herself to wonder what it would be like to be married to such a man. To share everything with him—share his bed. Then she forced herself to push those startling thoughts right out of her head. It was never going to happen; it was quite impossible. And once she had managed to convince herself of that she allowed herself to become angry at Sofia's insulting implication that she was quite incapable of running Dimitri's hotel.

'When Dimitri drew up his will, he wasn't matchmaking. He was concerned only about the future of his hotel,' she said fiercely. 'And I intend to justify his decision to put me in charge, once I've learnt everything I need to know. But if you're still worried about the amount of time I'll be spending with Nikolaos, here's something that might make you feel a lot better about it. If Dimitri *did* have any plans to force us into some kind of relationship, they are most certainly not going to work. I would rather die and go to hell than marry Nikolaos Konstantin!' Emily was well aware that she was speaking more out of bravado than conviction now. She also rather desperately needed to escape from the increasingly claustrophobic atmosphere inside the car. She scrambled out and slammed the door. Then she turned back to Sofia. 'You can tell Nikolaos that I intend to walk back to the hotel,' she added tensely. 'I don't want to spend one more minute today with any members of the Konstantin family!'

When she got back to the hotel, she went straight up to her room, locked the door, and finally found some relief in a great flood of tears. She seemed to be crying over so many things. Her loss of her mother from a severe stroke. Unusual in someone of her age, the doctors had told them, but it happened. Then, just a few months later, the devastating discovery that Dimitri was seriously ill. His illness had progressed with terrifying speed. Emily had given up her own flat, taken extended compassionate leave from her job, and moved back into her family home so that she could

elp to nurse him through those last few weeks. And
now they were both gone, and she was left with such
an awful sense of loneliness, a frightening lack of
control over the situation she now found herself in, and
growing trepidation about the future.

When the tearing sobs finally subsided to a few
hiccups, Emily was so exhausted that she slept for a
while. When she finally woke up again, she was still
tired but felt much less depressed, as if the tears had
washed away much of her sadness. An almost cold
shower livened her up still further, and she realised she
was beginning to feel hungry. She didn't quite feel up
to a solitary meal in the hotel dining-room, though,
and so phoned Room Service and asked for a simple
supper to be brought to her room.

After she had eaten, she went to bed and slept very
soundly. She finally drifted into a much lighter sleep
just after dawn, and was eventually woken up by a
discreet knock on the door. Emily rubbed her eyes,
blinked a few times, and then saw that a young maid
had come in and was beginning to gather her clothes
from the wardrobe. She immediately sat up in bed,
much more fully awake.

'What are you doing?' she asked, in a puzzled voice.
I think you must have the wrong room.'

'No, this is the right room,' said the maid a little
nervously. 'I'm following orders from Mr Konstantin —
you have to move out.'

Emily blinked. Nikolaos was throwing her out of the
hotel? But why? Because of yesterday? Had Sofia told
him what had happened after he had left the two of
them in the car? Or was it because she had had the
temerity to threten him with legal action? He most
certainly hadn't liked that!

She scrambled out of bed and hurried into the

bathroom. First, she had to get dressed; then, she intended to confront Nikolaos Konstantin. He probably wouldn't want to listen to her, but she was determined to let him know, in no uncertain terms, her opinion of a man who would throw a lone woman out on to the street just because she had had the nerve to stand up to him!

She took the lift up to the penthouse suite and then marched along to his office, going straight past his secretary, who made a couple of flustered attempts to stop her. Emily threw open Nikolaos's door, walked in, and then planted herself in front of his desk, her blue eyes blazing down into his own dark, short-tempered gaze.

'I thought that, if you were nothing else, at least you were a gentleman!' she accused furiously.

His secretary, who had scurried into the room after her, looked askance. Nikolaos flicked a quick glance at her, and then gave a curt nod. 'It's all right, I'll take care of this,' he said shortly.

His secretary scuttled out of the room again, looking extremely relieved. This obviously wasn't a situation that happened too often, and she clearly didn't feel confident of dealing with it.

Nikolaos's dark gaze swivelled back to rest on Emily's face. She nearly flinched under the intense scrutiny of those almost black eyes, but forced herself to stand up defiantly straight.

'I'm busy,' he said crisply. 'Whatever you have to say to me, please keep it brief.'

'Oh, I'll keep it very brief,' she retorted. 'In fact, I can say it in one sentence. I am *not* going to let you throw me out on to the street! At least, not until I've had a chance to find alternative accommodation.'

Nikolaos looked bemused. 'I don't have the slightest ea what you're talking about!'

'You're making me leave this hotel,' Emily said cusingly.

'Yes, I am. I'm moving you to Limassol.'

'Moving—moving me to Limassol?' Emily echoed, r tone much less confrontational.

'Bringing you here was only a temporary arrange- ent. I thought you understood that.'

'How could I? No one bothered to tell me about it.'

'The mistake seems to have been mine. I apologise r it,' he said formally.

Emily nearly fell over backwards in surprise. ikolaos Konstantin apologising for something? That d to be a first! She supposed that she ought to spond to it in some way, though.

'In that case—I apologise as well,' she said rather ffly. 'I shouldn't have burst in and accused you like at. I should have given you a chance to explain why u wanted me to leave the hotel.'

'Yes, you should have,' he agreed coolly. 'But since e now seem to be discussing the subject in a more lult fashion, do you have any objections to being oved to Limassol?'

'Well—no——' she said, half wishing that she could ink of a reasonable objection. 'Except that I don't derstand *why* I have to be moved.'

'I needed to be in Larnaca for a few days for business asons, and it made sense to bring you with me, since u know no one else on the island. My hotel in massol is where I intend you should begin your aining, though. Once you've had a good grounding in tel management, we will then move on to Paphos, here Dimitri's hotel is situated.'

'I wish you'd told me all of this,' Emily said with a

fresh touch of annoyance. Really, the man was qui
impossible! He arrogantly made plans without consul
ing anyone.

'I believe I've already apologised for that,' Nikolao
said more coolly, without a trace of genuine apology i
his tone.

'Are you sure that you're not keeping me in the dai
on purpose?' she said suspiciously.

'I don't have the time to play such childish games.
promised Dimitri that I will do for you what he one
did for me, and I will keep that word.'

Emily looked at him with fresh curiosity. 'What h
once did for you? What do you mean?'

Nikolaos looked as if he regretted having made tha
admission. After a brief pause, though, he said, 'Whe
I was quite young, my father's health became bad, an
I had to take over his business affairs. Dimitri taug
me all that I needed to know, and provided the suppo
that I needed in those early days. I will now do th
same for you. What you do with that knowledge wi
then be your affair.'

'You must have been very fond of your uncle,' Emi
said slowly.

'Yes, I was. Which is why, even though I disapprove
of his remarriage to your mother, I agreed to incorpo
ate his hotel into my chain and run it for him while h
lived in England. Why I agreed to the terms of his will

Emily began to understand the conflict that la
behind the hostility he so often showed to her. H
deep affection for Dimitri had made him make
promise that he was honour-bound to keep, eve
though he had no wish to.

'You do realise that, at the end of the year, his hot
will belong to me?' she said, wanting to get everythin

perfectly straight between them. 'Whether you think I'm capable of running it or not?'

'I accept that you are Dimitri's legal heir,' he said shortly. 'Although I sometimes wonder how you managed that,' he added, his dark eyes narrowing. 'I suppose that it probably wasn't too difficult. Dimitri was already very ill and at a low ebb when he drew up that will — and he always had a weakness for beautiful women.'

Shock hit her as she realised just what he was insinuating.

'That is a terrible thing to say!' she got out in a choked voice, hardly able to speak.

He was unmoved by her emotional response. 'Is it? It's a fact that beautiful women find it far easier than plain ones to get what they want.'

That was the second time he had called her beautiful. It threw Emily even further off balance; she was still angry, but now she was confused as well; he couldn't *really* think she was beautiful — could he? Or was he doing it on purpose? Was he deliberately trying to make her feel mixed up, because it made her easier to handle?

She knew that she needed to retreat, get herself together again. She backed towards the door, realising that she had had as much as she could cope with of Nikolaos Konstantin for one day!

His black gaze glittered scathingly, as if he knew very well that she was running away, but right now she didn't care. Getting away from his domineering presence was the only thing of any importance at the moment. Emily left his office, didn't even look at Nikolaos's secretary as she hurried past her desk, and went straight back to her room.

Once she reached it, she found herself moving over

to the mirror and staring at her reflection. She studied her astonishingly blue eyes; the glossy gold coils of her hair; the shape of her face, much thinner than it used to be because the sudden, awful loss of her mother and Dimitri had taken its toll, and yet the new thinness suited her; it emphasised the fine bone-structure that lay underneath. Then she gazed at her mouth, her lips a little moist where she had nervously licked them.

She realised that she didn't look quite as drawn, as pale as she had a couple of days ago, as if the gentle sun of Cyprus had already worked a little magic. But beautiful? Emily gazed at herself wonderingly, unable to decide. And she was more certain than ever that Nikolaos couldn't have meant it when he had used that emotive word. His taste surely couldn't run to her English rose kind of looks? He would be drawn to the dark, sultry, sun-kissed women of his island—someone like his cousin Sofia.

Emily suddenly shook her head, as if trying to wake herself from a dream. This was ridiculous, she told herself firmly. All this because of a word that had probably been no more than a slip of the tongue. And if he *had* used it on purpose, then it had been because he had wanted to confuse her. And how pleased he would be if he ever found out how well he had succeeded!

She forced herself away from the mirror, and began to make a start on her packing. It was time to be the old, sensible, capable Emily again, the one who had learnt to cope with most of life's problems, thanks to Dimitri's influence. And if she sometimes felt as if that old Emily was slowly falling apart, with little chance of putting her back together again, then she was determined that no one else would know about it.

When she was ready to leave, she found that

Nikolaos's car was waiting outside the hotel, to take her and her luggage to Limassol. There was no sign of Nikolaos himself, though. Instead, the chauffeur loaded her luggage into the boot, courteously opened the door for her, and then drove her to Limassol.

It was a much larger town than Larnaca, but one thing was the same — Nikolaos's hotel occupied a prime site on the seafront. And, once again, Emily found that she had been given a suite of rooms with gorgeous views. The promenade and the wide expanse of Akrotiri Bay stretched out in front of her windows, and the rooms themselves were spacious and luxurious. She supposed that it was because she was part of the Konstantin family — although Nikolaos certainly wished that she weren't — that she had been given this preferential treatment.

Once she had finished unpacking, Emily wandered down to the hotel restaurant and ordered a light lunch. She had no plans for the afternoon, but she knew that she had had enough of sitting around, doing nothing. She wanted to get down to some serious work. As soon as Nikolaos arrived, she would ask him when her training could start. If only she didn't have to work under *him*, she told herself with a small grimace. That was the one big drawback to all the arrangements that Dimitri had made!

She found herself remembering Sofia's accusation that Dimitri had thrown her and Nikolaos together deliberately, in the hope that some kind of romance would blossom. Emily found herself giving a small grimace. Even if that *had* been Dimitri's intention — and she didn't believe, for one moment, that it had been — it was a plan that had been doomed to total failure from the very start.

She was just drinking a cup of sweet black coffee at

the end of her meal when a tall, good-looking man came over. 'I am the hotel manager, Alexandros Stavrolakis,' he introduced himself. 'Mr Konstantin asked me to take care of you personally. Is everything satisfactory?'

'Yes, quite satisfactory,' she said. 'But isn't Mr Konstantin here, at the hotel?'

'I believe he has business commitments elsewhere,' said the manager. 'We are expecting him in a couple of days.'

'Oh,' said Emily, disappointed. It looked as if she would have to wait to begin work.

'Mr Konstantin wanted me to tell you about the carnival,' the manager went on. 'Today is the day of the big parade. He thought that you might like to attend, if you have no other plans. Everyone goes to the Limassol carnival,' the manager told her with growing enthusiasm. 'There are lots of bands and floats, and everyone has a good time. And tonight, at the hotel, there will be a masquerade ball. All guests at the hotel are welcome, and the hire of a costume for the evening can be arranged.'

'I'm not sure about the ball, but I'd certainly like to go to the carnival,' Emily said at once.

'You'll enjoy it,' he promised her. 'And you must come to the ball as well. A pretty girl like you will have a lot of fun.'

But Emily wasn't sure that she was entitled to have fun yet. It didn't seem right; she felt as if she still ought to be in mourning. And yet both her mother and Dimitri had been people who had enjoyed their lives to the full once they were back together again — she knew that they wouldn't have wanted her to shut herself away, to go on feeling sad and depressed for month after lonely, empty month.

She decided to think about the ball later. She would definitely go to the carnival, though, and she was aware of a sense of anticipation as she left the hotel and stepped out into the bright sunshine.

She found that the carnival route was already lined with crowds of noisily cheerful people. The floats had already begun to trundle past, and Emily pushed through to the front to get a better view.

The carnival turned out to be a noisy, cheerful, colourful spectacle. Great papier mâché figures perched precariously on the floats, and looked as if they might topple off at any moment into the crowds of laughing people. The figures had been decorated in brilliantly coloured costumes, and had huge, grinning, and sometimes grotesque heads. Emily found herself actually grinning back at an enormous jester with red and yellow trousers, great red pointed shoes, and brightly patterned cape. Other floats had been decorated with oversized birds or animals, people danced and sang, music blared out as bands marched past, and children looked adorable in their carefully made costumes. The atmosphere was relaxed and carefree, and Emily loved every moment of it. She had been afraid that, going on her own, she might feel rather lonely, but everyone was so friendly, the people all around her talked to her, and she was made to feel part of the festivities.

When the parade was finally over, she found herself singing under her breath as she made her way back to the hotel. It was a very long time since she had felt this good.

Alexandros Stavrolakis was standing in the lobby as she went in, and he immediately smiled at her.

'Did you enjoy the carnival, Miss Peterson?'

'Oh, yes,' she said, her face still glowing.

'And now you want to choose your costume for the masquerade ball tonight?'

Buoyed up by the feeling of light-heartedness that had come over her during the carnival, Emily nodded her head.

'Yes, I do.'

The manager led her to a side-room, where a selection of costumes had been laid out. Other guests were already there, choosing their costumes, and there was a lot of laughter and teasing as people picked up outfits that were obviously wildly unsuitable. Quite a few of them spoke to Emily, either asking for advice or offering it, and she easily joined in the relaxed, friendly atmosphere. She finally chose a dress for herself that was based on a medieval design, with a fitted bodice, square neckline and long, loose, flowing sleeves. It was a dark, rich red in colour, and a sequinned mask completed the outfit.

She went up to her room, showered and washed her hair, and then let her hair dry in a loose riot of gold curls. She had to admit to a distinct flutter of excitement as she finally put on the long red dress. She used a dark gloss on her lips to intensify their colour, and her blue eyes sparkled behind the sequinned mask.

When she finally made her way back downstairs, the ball was already under way. Music throbbed through the large room where it was being held, the lighting was subdued, and costumed figures whirled round the dance-floor.

Suddenly shy, Emily stood inside the doorway for a couple of minutes and found herself wishing that Nikolaos were here, not because she wanted to go to this ball with him—of *course* she didn't, she told herself firmly—but at least his would have been a familiar face. Soon, though, a man with a friendly smile and eyes that were warm and kind behind the silk mask he wore, came up to her and whisked her off on to the dance-floor.

As soon as the dance was over, another masked and costumed man eagerly took his place, and it soon became clear that she wasn't going to be short of partners that night. Smiling men introduced themselves, carried her off to dance, and offered to get her food and drink. Some were expert dancers, others trampled all over her feet, apologising charmingly. Emily didn't mind; her shyness had worn off now and she was thoroughly enjoying herself and glad that she had decided to come.

As the evening wore on, she sometimes exchanged light kisses with her partners at the end of a dance. The kisses didn't mean anything, they were simply a friendly exchange, part of the carnival spirit. Most of the men were here with their wives, and any flirting was very light-hearted.

The hours slid by, midnight came and went, the lights were turned down even lower and the atmosphere became more intimate and seductive. Emily decided that it was time for her to leave. The last kiss she had received had been a little more serious than the others, and she didn't want to get involved in any complications of that kind. She was still flushed and hot from being whirled round the dance-floor, though, and she wanted one last cooling drink before she left, a fruit juice this time, because she had already drunk too much of the legendary Cyprus wine and she knew that it was beginning to go to her head.

Before she could get herself a drink, however, strong arms suddenly locked around her and she found herself being swept back on to the dance-floor. Her new partner was tall, and a black silk mask hid most of his face. She smiled up at him in the semi-darkness and waited for him to introduce himself, but he didn't say a word as he expertly guided her round the floor. One of his hands pressed lightly against the small of her back, the other held her fingers in an unexpectedly tight grip.

Emily discovered that she was beginning to feel slightly dizzy. She didn't know if it was from the heat, or the rather stifling presence of her partner. He seemed to be having a rather odd effect on her breathing; perhaps it was because he was holding her much more tightly than any of her other partners had done. She found herself almost gasping for breath as he drew her still closer, the music little more than a dull thud in her ears. Or was it the thud of her heart? And her hand felt hot against his, so hot, as if there were small flames dancing over her fingertips and across her palm.

The music slowed, became more smoochy. His body moved against hers in a sensual rhythm and, to her alarm, she found herself responding. Her feet barely seemed to touch the floor, her skin burned, she felt as if she *had* to get some air or she would simply collapse into his arms. But they were very strong arms, and she was sure that they wouldn't let her fall; she could feel the strength of his muscles against her —

Then the dance was suddenly over. Emily felt both relieved and yet oddly agitated. Who *was* he? Would he leave her now, and find another partner? Still without saying a single word to her? And would he give her a friendly parting kiss, as several of the other men had done?

She found herself shivering at the prospect. Yet it was a strange kind of shiver, almost of excitement. She couldn't remember ever feeling a sense of terrified expectancy quite like this. And then he *was* kissing her, but it wasn't like any other kiss she had received tonight.

Swift, deep, intense, punishing—and then it was over. Emily could feel herself shaking. Then the trembling increased as her partner finally spoke.

'Did you enjoy that, Emily?' said Nikolaos Konstantin's voice harshly. 'And do you intend to kiss every man in this room tonight, and drag the reputation of the Konstantin family right through the gutter?'

He whipped off his mask, and Emily found herself staring straight into Nikolaos's dark, glittering eyes. She couldn't say anything, couldn't move. And then, as if he couldn't help himself, he suddenly bent his head and kissed her again.

CHAPTER FOUR

THE second kiss was as intense as the first, and Emily had the strange impression that it had shocked him almost as much as it had her. Then Nikolaos released her, took a step back, and stared down at her.

She still couldn't get out a single word. She seemed to have been totally paralysed by that kiss.

His dark eyes remained fixed on her, seeming to be boring right inside her head. Then, with an obvious effort, he tore his gaze away.

'I want to see you first thing in the morning,' he said tautly. 'Be in my office at eight o'clock.'

He turned round and strode off, and Emily didn't begin to breathe normally again until he had left the room and was completely out of sight.

Shaken and wide-eyed, she made her own way towards the door. As far as she was concerned, the masquerade ball was definitely over! She licked her dry lips, but then hurriedly stopped because she thought that she could still taste him.

Stop it, that kiss wasn't important, wasn't important, *wasn't important*, she told herself over and over as she hurried up to her room. It would never have happened at all if she had realised that it was Nikolaos she was dancing with.

Why hadn't she recognised him? she wondered. Of course, there had been the darkness, the heat, the music — and that black mask that had covered most of his face. But she should have known it was him; something should have told her, warned her —

Back in her room, she stripped off the dark red dress, tossed it over the chair, and hurried into the shower. She turned the setting right down, and let the cool water cascade over her hot skin until it made her shiver. Then she got into bed, and tried to sleep.

It was impossible, of course. Emily kept remembering that she had an appointment with Nikolaos at eight o'clock the following morning. Every time she thought about it, her nerves gave a sharp twinge and she would begin to toss restlessly again.

By the time the sun finally came up in the morning, she had slept for no more than a couple of hours, and then only fitfully. She crawled out of bed, examined her pale face and heavy eyes in the mirror, and gave a grimace. She wasn't going to dazzle anyone with her looks today!

She didn't bother to dress up for the interview. Instead, she pulled on a loose jogging suit and wriggled her feet into a pair of trainers. After she had endured Nikolaos's lecture—and she was absolutely sure that was why he had summoned her to his office this morning, to let her know in no uncertain terms what he thought about her behaviour last night—she would go for a run. Although not fanatical about keeping fit, she found that a leisurely run helped her to relax. And she was absolutely sure that she would *need* something to help her relax by the time Nikolaos had finished with her!

With her head held at a defiant angle—although she didn't feel in the least defiant inside—she made her way to his office, knocked briskly on the door and then walked inside.

She immediately felt at a disadvantage because Nikolaos was dressed very formally this morning, in a light-coloured and immaculately cut suit. A paper-thin

gold watch glittered on his wrist, and the crisp white-
ness of his shirt made his hair and eyes seem even
blacker than usual. In contrast, she felt distinctly under-
dressed in her old jogging suit.

That made her more antagonistic than she had
intended. 'Well?' she said, almost challengingly. 'Here
I am.'

She tensely waited for him to bring up the subject of
last night. And those two kisses — what would he say
about *them*? Emily found that she was inwardly trembling as she waited for the lecture to begin.

Instead, though, Nikolaos said in a crisp tone, 'I've
decided that it's time you started work.'

Emily blinked in surprise. 'Work?' she repeated,
caught completely off balance — as he had no doubt
intended.

'It is why you're here,' he reminded her, although
with absolutely no trace of the sarcasm she might have
expected. His gaze briefly flicked over her. 'You'll need
to wear something more suitable.'

'I — I was going for a run.' She was still flustered. He
wasn't going to mention last night? Not say anything
about it *at all*?

Apparently not, because his voice remained crisp
and impersonal as he spoke again.

'I suggest that you go for your run, shower, and then
change into something more suitable. Be back here in
an hour. Then we'll discuss how you can most usefully
spend your time over the next few months.'

'Oh — yes — right,' Emily managed to get out, still
not quite believing that he wasn't going to say one
single word about the masquerade ball. Nikolaos had
begun to flick through some papers on his desk, though,
clearly indicating that this particular conversation was
at an end. She backed out of his office, took a deep

breath, and finally began to relax just a fraction. Perhaps he was simply so busy that he had forgotten about last night, she told herself hopefully. Then she shook her head. Although she couldn't have explained why, she was quite certain that he *hadn't* forgotten those kisses. He had obviously decided to ignore them, however. He intended to behave as if they hadn't even happened.

Emily was very happy to go along with that. She certainly hadn't forgotten them, either, but she was sure that she could, given time. At least, that was what she told herself. Anyway, it wouldn't happen again, so it wouldn't be a problem.

She decided to skip the run. She went straight back to her room, showered, and then put on a straight, dark skirt with a rather prim white blouse. There wasn't very much she could do with her hair — the glossy gold curls had always had a mind of their own — but she clipped it back from her face with a couple of plain slides, and then used soft, subtle colours to tone down the vivid blue of her eyes, and the redness of her lips where she had bitten them nervously.

She took one last look in the mirror, and wrinkled her nose. 'You look like Miss Plain Jane, the perfect secretary,' she told herself. 'But at least Nikolaos won't be able to complain about the way you look!'

Emily tried to convince herself that she felt relaxed and confident as she went back down to Nikolaos's office. The truth was that she felt very *unrelaxed*. He seemed to be able to do that to her with such ease; make her feel about sixteen again, a young girl trying to act like a grown-up.

Nikolaos glanced up as she walked in, and then shot a swift second glance at her, obviously momentarily startled by the change in her appearance. He didn't comment on it, though. Instead, he briskly indicated that she should sit in the chair on the other side of the desk.

'A year is an extremely short time to learn everything you need to know,' he began without preamble. 'If you're serious about wanting to take over the running of Dimitri's hotel, then you'll have to work very hard, and for long hours.'

'I'm serious,' Emily assured him, without hesitation. 'And I'll work as long and as hard as necessary. I'm looking forward to it, especially learning about the financial side. You know that I'm training to be an accountant. Dealing with all the varied finances of a hotel will be very good work experience.'

Nikolaos looked at her thoughtfully for a while, his dark, intense gaze making her want to squirm in her seat, but Emily forced herself to sit very still. Finally, he gave a brief nod.

'I see no reason why you shouldn't start right now. I'll arrange for the manager to show you the accounts for this particular hotel. Once you fully understand where the profits — and losses — come from, everything will become much clearer. What you'll then need is practical experience — which I intend to give you. And one more thing. Don't expect to be treated leniently or granted special favours because of who you are,' he warned.

'I don't expect any such thing,' she said rather indignantly.

'Then I suggest you begin work,' he said.

From the gleam in his eyes, Emily guessed that he intended to work her much harder than the other members of his staff. He wanted to push her to the limits, to see what she was capable of — or if she would crack.

But she certainly wasn't going to crack, she told herself with some determination. This was a challenge that she fully intended to see through to the end. And she had the feeling that, although Nikolaos would work her until she was just about ready to drop, he would also be fair. He would never push her *too* far, beyond all reasonable limits.

Emily left his office with a new sense of confidence. She felt as if she was taking the first steps towards getting her life back together. She would be working again, doing something positive, and she was sure that she could make a success of this. She certainly wanted to, for herself as well as for Dimitri.

During the next few weeks, she certainly worked harder than she had ever done during her life before. The financial side was easy; Emily had a natural aptitude for figures, she could read a balance sheet as easily as a newspaper headline. Once she had studied the accounts and balance sheets, though, and understood how all the different financial sections of the hotel fitted together, Nikolaos began to make sure that she had some practical experience. He took her round each part of the hotel, introduced her to the staff, and explained clearly and in detail how everything worked and meshed together. Under his close supervision, she spent time on the reception desk, dealt with reservations and the payment of bills, learnt how the bar and restaurant dealt with the sudden rush of customers at mealtimes, and toured the small shops situated on the ground floor which provided additional services for hotel guests — hairdressers and beauty parlours, elegant designer clothes and jewellery.

Then Nikolaos took her behind the scenes, so that she appreciated the importance of the hotel porters, the bellboys, the housekeeper and the room maids.

And her new experiences weren't confined to the hotel; he took her with him to various business meetings. Emily was fascinated by the way he dominated those meetings, putting his ideas forward with power and clarity, winning people round to his point of view with sudden flashes of devastating charm. She also began to learn a lot more about his business interests, since he had decided that she needed more all-round experience. He took her to one of his vineyards, where she spent several absorbing hours learning about the production of wine. On another occasion, they stopped for lunch in a high-class restaurant which specialised in Cypriot dishes. Here, Nikolaos introduced her to the *meze*, a great array of dips with sesame seed bread, salads, smoked sausages, marinated ham, vine leaves stuffed with rice and lamb, charcoal-grilled pork, ewe's-milk cheese, and a dozen more tantalising dishes.

'Try as many as you like and eat as much as you want,' Nikolaos told her, and Emily, starving hungry, did her best to obey. It wasn't until the end of the meal, when she overheard a conversation between Nikolaos and the head waiter, that she realised Nikolaos owned the restaurant. And that it was apparently only one of a large chain he owned all over the island.

Every night, she tumbled into bed and slept like a log, totally exhausted but satisfied by what she had accomplished that day. She was very aware that Nikolaos's dark eyes were fixed on her much of the time, watching and assessing her. Sometimes, she thought that he was waiting for her to make a major mistake. Or just give up, because she couldn't cope with the pressure of work.

But Emily did neither of those things. Oh, she certainly made small mistakes, but because the rest of the staff in the hotel were friendly and helpful she quickly managed to put most of them right. And she got on well with the staff; they laughed and joked with her, sometimes in English and sometimes in Greek, which Emily spoke rather haltingly, although with increasing confidence as she practised. She had learned some basic Greek from Dimitri, although this was the first chance she had really had to use it.

As she gradually began to understand how all the different sections of hotel work meshed together, she became more and more fascinated by it. So many people, all doing different jobs, and yet all with the same aim in mind — to provide first-class accommodation and service for the guests who came to visit this beautiful island. And the guests themselves were endlessly changing, providing even more variety. Some were pleasant and appreciative of how hard the staff worked, others were far more demanding, a few downright rude and even aggressive. Emily learnt how to soothe ruffled guests, and keep her own temper at the same time, even on the rare occasions when they actually became abusive. And Nikolaos eventually let her take complete charge of different sections of the hotel for a few days at a time, so that she understood the different problems that the management staff had to face.

She had very little free time, but after a week when she had put in particularly long hours Nikolaos turned the car off the main road on the way back from a business meeting which they had both attended, and headed up into the hills. Emily looked at him in surprise, but when he offered no explanation she simply sat back, relaxed, and began to enjoy the peace of the countryside, and the caressing heat of the sun. She realised that the Cypriot spring had crept over the island, almost unnoticed, while she had been working so very hard. There had been a steady, gentle rise in the temperature, and the countryside was now bursting into great sheets of colour as the spring flowers blossomed in the bright, warm sunshine. Fields of scarlet poppies and yellow daisies dazzled her eyes as Nikolaos drove along the narrow roads, rockroses tumbled down the hillsides, clumps of wallflowers and blue irises stood out vividly against the green of the grass. And the citrus trees were in bloom now, their scent seeming to drift everywhere, turning the air of the entire island deliciously fragrant.

Nikolaos drove to a small village in the hills behind Limassol. He negotiated a series of spectacular hairpin bends at a speed which made Emily nervously half close her eyes, but she needn't have worried; he swung the large car expertly round the tight corners and then brought it to a halt on the outskirts of the village. They spent a pleasant half an hour wandering through the quiet streets of the village, finally stopping at a taverna for a glass of light, sparkling white wine. The owner entertained them with a tale of a huge snake which allegedly lived in the local cemetery and went for walks around the village at night. He looked a little disappointed when his famous tale of the snake didn't make Emily shiver, but she had never been scared of anything that wriggled or crawled. She simply grinned and told the owner of the taverna that it was a pity the snake didn't go for its stroll during the day. Then it could be seen and photographed by tourists, and become a celebrity.

When they finally got back into the car and headed back to the hotel, Emily realised the reason for the unexpected trip. Nikolaos had needed to relax for a couple of hours, to take a break from the gruelling schedule that he set himself. But why had he taken her with him? she wondered curiously. Surely he didn't find her a relaxing person to be with?

On the other hand, they had worked together surprisingly well over the past few weeks. There had been very little friction or argument, with the only nerve-jarring moments — on Emily's part, at least — coming on those occasions when she found herself physically close to him. He could still play havoc with all her nerve-ends just by standing next to her, but she knew that she had kept her reactions well under control and there was no reason for him to suspect that she found his physical presence so very disturbing.

When they arrived back at the hotel, there was an urgent phone call for Nikolaos. When he had taken it, he came back to her with a light frown on his face. 'That was the night manager,' he told her. 'He's unwell, and won't be able to work his next few shifts.' He paused for a moment as if turning something over in his mind, then he said decisively, 'I want you to take over his duties until he's fit to return to work.'

Emily blinked. 'You mean that I'll be completely in charge? Of the whole hotel? All night?' She knew that she was gabbling a little, but she was so surprised that she just couldn't help it.

'If you think you can handle the responsibility.'

'Yes, I can,' she said at once, hoping that she could live up to the confident note in her voice.

'You shouldn't run into any major problems. The hotel's usually fairly quiet at night.'

'Even if there are problems, I'll cope with them,' Emily said firmly. She was determined to prove to Nikolaos that she was capable and competent, and that she had benefitted hugely from her intensive training over the past few weeks.

Nikolaos looked at her assessingly for a few moments; then he gave a brief nod, and walked away.

Emily went straight up to her room to get herself ready. When she glanced in the mirror, she saw that her eyes were shining with excitement. To be in charge of this large hotel, even if was only during the night, when things were much less hectic than in the day-time — it was both an exciting and terrifying prospect. She was sure that she was ready for this kind of responsibility, though, and she was certainly looking forward to it.

She was almost disappointed when the evening went very smoothly, with no crises for her to deal with. The restaurant slowly emptied as guests drifted up to their rooms, the bar closed and takings were counted, then sent to the accounts manager. There had been a small private dinner party in one of the hotel's special function rooms, and Emily made a point of saying goodnight personally to the guests, and discreetly checking that they had enjoyed their evening and had no complaints. After that, the hotel slowly became very quiet as the staff who had been on the evening shift went home and the guests settled down for the night.

Lights were switched off in the restaurant, bar, kitchens and function rooms, leaving only the main reception area staffed and lit. Emily began to make her way back to the small office she was using, intending to get on with some paperwork, but then heard her name being called by Maria, the girl on the reception desk.

As she went over, she could see that Maria looked worried. 'What is it?' Emily asked.

'There's a disturbance on the second floor,' Maria told her. 'Room twenty-two. Some of the guests in the nearby rooms have been phoning down and complaining; they say that it's keeping them awake.'

'All right, I'll deal with it,' Emily said at once.

'Shall I ask one of the night porters to come up with you?'

'No,' Emily said, after a moment's thought. 'I can always send for them, if I need them. I'll just go up and see what the problem is. Who's in room twenty-two?'

'A Mr Ron Carson. He checked in late this afternoon; he's here for a few days on a business trip.'

'On his own?'

Maria nodded.

'Then perhaps the problem is that he's found company since he arrived, and is having a small private party,' Emily said drily. 'I'll turf out anyone who shouldn't be in that room, and politely remind him that other people are trying to sleep.'

'Be careful,' Maria warned.

'Don't worry, I'll be fine,' Emily assured her.

'Are you *sure* you don't want to take one of the night porters with you?'

'No, I'm going to try and handle the situation myself. It'll be good practice; it's the kind of thing that happens now and again in hotels, and I need experience in coping with it.'

Maria looked doubtful, but Emily gave her a reassuring smile and then ran quickly and confidently up the stairs. Be polite but firm, she instructed herself. She was sure that Mr Carson would be willing to listen to reason.

As she approached room twenty-two, she soon realised why the guests in the adjoining rooms were complaining. She could hear loud, tuneless singing in a deep male voice, stopping for a few moments and then starting up again, the same song, as if the singer didn't know any other.

Emily knocked lightly on the door; then, when he

obviously didn't hear, rapped more loudly. The door
to the next room opened and an irate guest peered out.
'About time,' he grumbled. 'This has been going on for
ages.'

'I'm very sorry, I'm going to put a stop to it right
now,' Emily told him. 'Please go back to bed, and
accept my apologies for the disturbance.'

The guest looked slightly placated and disappeared
back into his own room. Emily knocked on Mr Carson's
door one more time, then tried the handle. It turned
easily, the door wasn't locked. Cautiously, she pushed
it open and went inside.

The room was medium-sized, and comfortably furnished with a double bed, an armchair, wardrobe and
plenty of cupboards. Mr Carson was sitting slumped in
the armchair, crooning softly to himself now. He
looked to be in his forties, rather overweight and very
red in the face. He was also obviously very drunk.

He looked up, saw her, and his expression immediately became belligerent.

'Who are you?' he demanded. 'And what are you
doing in my room?'

'My name is Emily Peterson,' she told him. 'I'm the
night manager. Mr Carson, I'm afraid that we've been
getting a lot of complaints. You're making a great deal
of noise, and keeping some of our other guests awake.'

He took no notice of what she had said, but instead
just kept staring at her, his eyes a little wild and
unfocused. 'This is a private room,' he said at last, in
an angry tone. 'You've no right just to walk in here.'

'I've not only got the right to be here, I've also got
the right to ask you to leave if you continue to make a
disturbance,' Emily said, deliberately keeping her voice
very calm and courteous. 'It's late at night, Mr Carson,

and I think that it's time you stopped singing — and drinking — and tried to get some sleep.'

He got to his feet, and Emily involuntarily took a step backwards. He was a heavily built man, and suddenly looked very threatening. She began to regret her decision to come up here on her own, but told herself that now she was here she had to cope with the situation.

'Don't tell me what I can or can't do,' he said hostilely. 'I've paid for this room, I've got rights.'

Emily decided to try another tack. 'You're here on a business trip, aren't you, Mr Carson?'

'Yes, I am,' he said suspiciously. 'Not that that's any business of yours,' he added, glaring at her and swaying a little on his feet.

'You'll need a clear head if you've got meetings to attend and deals to negotiate. Why don't you sleep for a while? When you wake up in the morning, you'll feel refreshed and relaxed, and ready for work,' she said persuasively.

Ron Carson's eyes suddenly gleamed. 'You could help me relax,' he said in a slurred voice. 'A pretty girl like you — I'm sure that you'd be really good at something like that.'

Emily had enough common sense to realise that this situation was beginning to get out of hand. Never mind about her resolution to cope with it on her own, to prove that she could tackle any problems that came up. It was time to get some help.

She began to move towards the door. 'Where are you going?' Ron Carson demanded at once.

'I have to go and see someone,' Emily said, and this time it was a real effort to keep her voice sounding calm. 'I'll be back in just a few minutes.'

He suddenly lunged towards the door, moving with

surprising speed for someone so drunk. 'You're not walking out on me,' he shouted. 'Everyone walks out on me; even my wife walked out, said I was a rotten husband. I'm sick of it, it's got to stop, so you're staying right here!'

Emily's heart had begun to pound so loudly that it was making her feel slightly dizzy, but she knew she had to get out of this room. 'I won't be gone for long,' she tried to assure him shakily, but his arms were waving wildly now, he seemed to be losing all control.

'No,' he yelled, 'you're staying *here*; I'm going to make you stay.'

Emily ducked away from him; she had already decided to make a run for it; all she had to do was weave past him and get that door open. As she moved, though, one of his arms flailed round and hit her hard, knocking her off balance so that she nearly stumbled to the floor. Panic instantly shot through her, the fear of physical violence, a fear that had lain dormant for many years but suddenly flared into life again. She found herself seized by a crippling paralysis; she couldn't even seem to breathe and she certainly couldn't run.

Then the door was abruptly thrown open, a dark figure moved swiftly into the room, and only seconds later Ron Carson had been pinned down on the bed and was being held there by powerful arms.

Nikolaos briefly turned his head and looked at Emily, his black eyes brilliant with a mixture of anger and tension. 'Are you all right?' he demanded. 'Did he hurt you?'

Emily was sure that he was angry at *her* because she hadn't been able to control the situation. She tried to say something, but couldn't; her throat seemed to have seized up. And although she was sweating with fright she was also freezing cold; she could feel herself shivering violently.

Nikolaos held Ron Carson in place with just one hand while he reached for the phone. He spoke into it swiftly and curtly for just a few seconds. In no time at all, two of the night porters appeared at the door, and seized hold of Ron Carson.

'Take care of him,' Nikolaos said abruptly. 'You know what to do.' Then he turned back to Emily. 'Can you walk?'

Somehow, she found her voice again. 'Of course I can,' she croaked.

Her legs were still trembling so violently, though, that he had to hook one hand under her arm to keep her upright. He guided her along the corridor, past the wide-eyed guests who had come out to see what the commotion was all about, and then up in the lift to his suite of rooms at the very top of the hotel.

Emily had been to his office before, but not the rooms that were reserved for his own personal use. They were luxuriously furnished in plain colours, and he sat her in a soft leather armchair, then fixed his dark gaze on her again.

'All right,' he said in a rather grim tone, 'now tell me *exactly* what happened.'

'There—there were complaints of a disturbance in room twenty-two,' Emily said in a very quavery voice. 'I went up there and the man—he was drunk—and singing—and I explained that the other guests were trying to sleep, but he didn't care; then I tried to get help, but he closed the door. And his arms were swinging about, I got knocked——'

'He hit you?' Nikolaos cut in incredulously. For a moment, he looked so furious that Emily shrank back.

Then she realised that he wasn't angry at her; his fury was directed at the man who had behaved so loutishly.

'No—well, yes—he didn't mean to, I'm sure he didn't,' she said rather incoherently, her teeth beginning to chatter as she remembered all over again how frightened she had been, how terrified that, in a drunken temper, he would begin to hit her purposefully.

'Are you hurt?' he said quickly. 'Do you need a doctor?'

'No, no, I'm not hurt.'

His eyes remained locked on to her own hugely dilated pupils. 'But something's wrong. You must have seen men drunk before, most women have, you know how stupidly and irrationally they can behave. You had an extremely unpleasant experience tonight—and it could have been a great deal more unpleasant if Maria hadn't had the sense to phone me and tell me there was a problem—but you say that you're not hurt, and you've dealt with other problem guests over the past few weeks, and you coped with them very well. Why was tonight different? You were trembling from head to foot when I came into that room. You're still shaking,' he pointed out.

Emily managed to get a little control over her quivering limbs. 'I'm fine,' she mumbled.

'No, you're not.' He moved closer and looked at her more intensely. 'What's the matter with you, Emily?'

'I'm *all right*,' she insisted, frantically fighting back the fresh prickling of tears behind her eyes. She managed to get to her feet. 'I have to get back to my office; I'm still on duty.'

With the quick, easy movement of just one hand, Nikolaos forced her back into the armchair again.

'You're not leaving here until I find out what this is all about.'

'Look,' she said, making a huge effort to gather herself together, 'I had a bad experience, but it's over now, and I want to get back to work.'

'I'm taking you off duty for the rest of the night. And I think that someone should be with you. You're not in a fit state to be left on your own. I'll ask Maria to sit with you for a while.'

'I don't need anyone with me,' she said stubbornly.

Nikolaos sat down opposite her, and looked directly into her feverishly over-bright eyes.

'Why not?'

'Because —— ' she began. Then she clammed up. 'It's none of your business.'

'This is my hotel, that man was one of my guests, and I'm making it my business,' Nikolaos said tautly. 'I'm giving you two choices. Either you talk to me and tell me why you reacted so badly to what happened this evening, or I'm sending for a doctor. You're behaving very strangely, Emily.'

'I don't want a doctor,' she said at once. 'I don't want anyone to know —— '

'Know what?' Nicolaos questioned her relentlessly, his dark eyes still boring straight into her own.

'That — that I can still get upset over something like this,' she muttered at last.

He gave a quick frown. 'And what *did* upset you so much? The man's drunkenness?'

She shook her head. 'No,' she said in a low voice. She had to force the words out now. This was such a very private fear, something that she never spoke about to anyone. 'It was — it was the threat of violence. The way he hit me.'

'But you said it was accidental,' Nikolaos reminded her sharply. 'And that you weren't hurt.'

'Yes, but it — brought back bad memories,' she whispered, so quietly that he could only just hear her.

Nikolaos's eyes abruptly narrowed. 'Of someone who hit you on purpose?' he said in a harsh voice. 'And *did* hurt you?'

Emily didn't answer him. She couldn't seem to say any more. Even Dimitri hadn't known about it, and she and her mother had carefully avoided the subject for years.

'Who, Emily?' demanded Nikolaos. 'A lover?' Then his expression suddenly changed. 'Not Dimitri,' he said fiercely. 'Don't ever try and tell me that Dimitri would do something like that!'

'No, of course it wasn't Dimitri,' Emily said at once. 'He was one of the kindest, gentlest men I ever knew. It — it happened long before he came back into our lives. When I was young——'

A look of incredulity spread over Nikolaos's taut features. 'Your father?' he said in clear disbelief. 'Are you talking about your *father*?'

Emily realised that his was the automatic reaction of a Greek man who put the protection and love of his family before all else, and couldn't believe that another man would do otherwise. But she knew differently. Her head came up and she looked back at him defiantly. 'Do you think that I'm lying?' She pulled up the sleeve of her blouse. 'Feel my arm,' she said with some bitterness. '*Feel* it!'

His strong fingers ran over the smoothness of her skin, but then stopped at a certain point. 'There are old scars here,' he said slowly. 'And there's something wrong with the bone.'

'My father knocked me to the ground so hard that I broke my arm,' Emily said in a suddenly choked voice. 'The bone splintered, it wouldn't set properly afterwards. And something *inside* of me has never quite healed. Violence still frightens me, I hate it, hate it!'

And then, to her utter consternation, the tears she had been holding back so valiantly began to pour down her face in an unstoppable flood.

CHAPTER FIVE

NIKOLAOS'S face darkened, but his voice was unexpectedly gentle as he murmured to her soothingly, as he might have done to an upset child. Emily found herself supplied with a clean white handkerchief, and then his warm fingers gripped her hands until they stopped shaking. When the worst of the tears were over, he then coaxed her into drinking just enough brandy to help her get control of herself again.

When she finally looked at Nikolaos with her bruised, reddened eyes, though, she immediately shrank back when she saw the anger still clearly written on his face.

'I — I'm sorry,' she mumbled. 'I shouldn't have told you, shouldn't have made this embarrassing scene. It's nothing to do with you, not your problem.'

'Do you think I'm angry at *you*?' he said incredulously.

'Aren't you?' she said in a small voice.

'I'm angry at anyone, man or woman, who treats a child like that,' he said, in a barely controlled tone. 'That kind of abuse is quite unforgivable, there's nothing in this world that can excuse it.'

Emily gave a tired shake of her head. 'You can't say that; you don't know the circumstances ——'

'I don't need to know them,' he cut in, in a hard voice.

'He — my father — he wasn't like it all the time. And when something did happen he was always so sorry

86

fterwards. There were expensive toys, special reats —'

'Given out of guilt,' Nikolaos said ruthlessly.

Since Emily knew that was the truth, she didn't eply.

'Did you love him?' Nikolaos asked abruptly, a few moments later.

'I don't know,' Emily said softly. 'I tried to, I knew hat I ought to, he *was* my father. And when he died I vas sad, but there was also this enormous sense of elief. And that made me feel guilty for such a long, ong while, because I knew that I shouldn't feel like hat.'

'How did he die?'

'He worked on the oil rigs, there was an accident, an xplosion —'

'How old were you?'

'Ten. Nearly eleven.'

'That's a very impressionable age. How long had he een knocking you around?' Nikolaos asked with a lirectness that should have upset her all over again, nd yet didn't.

'I'm not sure. I can't quite remember. I suppose ince I was about five or six.'

Nikolaos muttered something almost violently under is breath.

'You're making it sound as if he did it all the time, ut he didn't,' Emily added defensively. 'And now that 'm older I can understand it more. My mother's second narriage — it wasn't happy. She married my father on he rebound, after she and Dimitri were divorced. She vas still in love with Dimitri, though, she never really oved anyone else. And my father must have known hat; I remember rows, accusations. And I don't hink —' Emily hesitated for a moment, because this was all getting far too personal, but she had bottled all of this up inside her for too long, she desperately needed to talk about it. 'I don't think that my mother would sleep with him for those last few years,' she blurted out. 'It made my father angry, frustrated, and he just lashed out blindly when it all got too much for him. And, sometimes, I just happened to be in the way.'

'You're making excuses for him,' Nikolaos said harshly. 'And what he did was quite indefensible.'

'No, I'm not making excuses,' Emily said in a low voice. 'I'm just saying that, now that I'm an adult, I understand better what can drive a man to behave like that. When I was a child, it was just — well, totally bewildering.'

'And frightening,' Nikolaos said, his tone still grim.

'Yes, very frightening,' she admitted softly. 'I didn't understand why it was happening, I kept thinking that I'd done something wrong, that it was somehow all my fault —'

'Your mother,' Nikolaos cut in, 'she must have known what was going on. Why the hell didn't she stop it?'

'Because she was frightened as well,' Emily said simply. 'He only hit me occasionally, but he hit her a lot, and sometimes hurt her quite badly.'

'She should have walked out, and taken you with her.'

'She was always sure that he would find her, no matter how far she ran. And my father always threatened that he would kill both of us, if he ever came home and found we weren't there.'

'What on earth made her marry a man like that?' Nikolaos demanded.

'My mother said that he wasn't like it when they first

married. It was only when the marriage started to go wrong that the violence started. Then he began drinking heavily, which made things much worse. I don't know what would have happened if he hadn't been killed in that accident. I think that my mother would have left him—she would have had to, to save her sanity. But if he'd found us I think he *might* have killed us. He was probably capable of it, when he was in one of his drunken tempers.'

Nikolaos was silent for quite some time. Then he finally said, 'I think you should get some rest. It's been a very long night. Do you want another brandy, to help you sleep?'

Emily shook her head. 'No. I think that I'll be all right now. I'm sorry that I've caused all this trouble.'

'You've caused me trouble since the day I first met you.' Yet his tone was unexpectedly soft, and when she got up and walked towards the door he followed her.

Emily found herself swallowing hard. Telling him all those intimate things about herself seemed to have forged some kind of link between them. And from the dark glow that suddenly shone in his eyes she knew that he was aware of it, too.

Nervously, she licked her lips, then realised almost at once that she shouldn't have done that. His gaze locked on to her soft, shining mouth, as if he would like to eat it. She felt her skin suddenly grow hot, and her breasts ached, as if they were being gently caressed. Yet he hadn't laid a finger on her, hadn't even tried to kiss her.

Nikolaos took an unexpectedly deep breath, and then stepped back from her. 'I'll arrange for you to work the late shift tomorrow, so that you can sleep late,' he said in a carefully controlled voice. 'Goodnight, Emily.'

'Goodnight,' she mumbled. Then she made herself walk away from his suite rather quickly, in case she was tempted to say — or do — something very silly. Like asking to stay a little longer. Asking to talk some more. And, perhaps, not only talk ——

Back in her own room, Emily showered and then got into bed. She felt much better than she had expected to feel. That flood of tears seemed to have finally washed away some of the bad memories of her frightening and often unhappy childhood. It was a long time before she got to sleep, though, and she had the feeling that it wasn't entirely because of that unpleasant encounter with Ron Carson. It had more to do with how much of herself she had revealed to Nikolaos. . .

When Emily finally opened her eyes again, she immediately remembered last night and tensed up a little. Then she slowly relaxed again as she realised that she was OK, she had laid some of the ghosts of her past to rest, and she was ready to move forward again. She peered at the clock beside her bed, then her pale gold eyebrows shot up. It was eleven o'clock! The morning was almost over.

She clambered out of bed and was just heading towards the bathroom when there was a knock on her door.

Oh, good, she thought, one of the staff was being kind enough to bring her some coffee. She hoped it was strong and sweet. She still felt sleepy and needed something to help her wake up!

Emily padded over to the door in her bare feet, and opened it. Then her sleepy eyes shot wide open as she found herself face to face with Nikolaos.

She could feel herself slowly going bright red. Too late, she remembered that she was only wearing a baggy cotton T-shirt, pulled on before she had crawled into bed last night. Right now, Emily wished that she was wearing a pair of very respectable pyjamas.

'I — er — I overslept,' she mumbled at last.

'So I see,' Nikolaos said drily. At the same time, his dark eyes fixed on her, and she was sure that they were taking in every detail, from her tousled blonde curls to her bare legs and feet.

'I d-don't usually open the door dressed like this,' she said, and she was annoyed to hear that slight stammer in her voice. She really had to get over this awful nervousness that he could so easily provoke in her. 'I thought — well, I thought it was one of the girls bringing me a cup of coffee.'

She fervently wished that he would stop looking at her. There was something about his eyes this morning that made all her nerve-ends twitch and jump uncomfortably. They glittered so very brightly, as if there were a small flame burning in their depths.

Nikolaos finally seemed to realise how intently he was staring at her. His face became more shuttered and his voice, when he finally spoke to her, was quite formal again.

'When you've dressed, I'd like you to come to my office,' he told her.

Emily started to say something but found that, for some strange reason, her throat had gone completely dry. She cleared her throat and tried again.

'I'll be there in ten minutes.'

This time, she managed not to stammer, but her voice was definitely quavery. What on earth's the matter with me this morning? she thought edgily.

Whatever it was, she was quite sure that it would improve considerably if Nikolaos would just turn round and walk away. Was he going to stand there all day, staring at her in that disturbingly intense way?

When he finally wheeled round and strode off, though, she was aware of a deep twinge of disappointment. She hurriedly closed the door, then leant against it, because she had discovered that her knees had gently begun to shake.

Why was she reacting like this? she wondered worriedly. And hadn't Nikolaos also been acting rather oddly? Really, everything had become very peculiar since yesterday. And she still couldn't quite believe that she had told Nikolaos all those extremely personal things about herself, actually talked to him about her father, confessed all the dark secrets of her childhood.

Emily shook her head. That encounter with the drunken Ron Carson must have affected her even more than she had realised, or she would never have told Nikolaos so many of her secrets. The fact that he now knew so much about her made her feel horribly vulnerable.

And she still had to cope with that summons to his office. What did he intend to say to her, when she got there? As Emily quickly showered and then dressed, she found that her legs still felt uncomfortably unsteady.

When she was finally ready, she took the lift up to his office. Then she paused outside the door for a few moments, to take a couple of deep breaths. Suddenly impatient with herself for letting him affect her like this, she tossed her head, sending rebellious gold curls dancing in all directions, opened the door, and quickly walked inside.

Nikolaos was sitting behind his desk, his features dark, his mouth set in a taut line.

'Take a seat,' he said, and something about his tone of voice made Emily immediately obey.

'After that incident last night, I want to lay down some rules for the future,' he went on. 'In future, if there are any reports of trouble in a guest's room, you will *not* go up there by yourself. Similarly, any cases of drunkenness in any part of the hotel will be dealt with by a male member of staff.'

But although this man could make her feel so vulnerable—and quite a lot of other things that were equally disturbing!—Emily wasn't ready to let him treat her like a child. 'Look, I know that I made a terrible mess of things last night,' she said, 'but if the same kind of situation comes up in the future I'm sure that I'll be able to cope with it.' She was determined not to let him use last night's fiasco as an excuse for branding her incompetent. She forced herself to give him a bright smile. 'I realise that I should have handled it differently from the very start, got help as soon as I saw the state Mr Carson was in. I've enough experience to know that you don't walk into that kind of situation on your own.'

His dark eyes bored into her. 'If last night is anything to go by, it seems that your experience of that kind of situation is extremely limited. In fact, for a girl of your age, you seem amazingly naïve about men and the way they can behave.'

'I don't think that I'm naïve,' she said indignantly. 'And I know about men, I've had boyfriends.'

'I wasn't talking about sexual experience,' Nikolaos said curtly, making her skin suddenly burn as she realised that she had made a bad mistake. 'Although if your behaviour on the night of the masquerade ball is anything to go by you're certainly not lacking in that.'

'What do you mean?' she said furiously.

His own black eyes had begun to glitter dangerously.

'Only that you kissed almost every man in the room. And appeared to enjoy it.'

'I did not kiss every man there,' Emily denied, in outrage. 'Just a few. And they were only friendly kisses! Except for——' She abruptly stopped, because she had been about to say, Except for the kisses that *you* gave me. Only that wouldn't have been wise. Not wise at all.

She was alarmed to find that Nikolaos's gaze had moved to her mouth as if he, too, was remembering those kisses. He got up from behind the desk, and she, too, jumped to her feet. The room suddenly seemed full of a tension that was quite unlike anything she had ever experienced before. The very air seemed to crackle with it; she could almost see the small electric sparks jumping between them.

'There's one easy way to find out just how experienced you are,' he said softly. And before Emily had a chance to ask nervously what it was he leant forward and slid his fingers through her bright gold curls so that they tumbled over his fingers; then he gripped them tightly, so that she couldn't pull away from him.

His mouth, when it closed over hers, was almost hard enough to hurt, experienced enough to know how to drown the fierceness of the kiss in a swift wave of pleasure. Emily had never been kissed like that in her life before; part of her shrank away from the sheer physical force of it, but another part of her seemed to flare into life as brand-new sensations rushed through her. It was the most terrifying thing that had ever happened to her, because she could feel herself losing control, and she had never done that with any man before.

The kiss went on and on, until she couldn't breathe, couldn't think, couldn't hear anything except the hard, erratic thumping of her heart. One of Nikolaos's hands remained tangled in her hair, making sure that she couldn't get away. The other slid over her bare wrist, moved up her arm; her skin felt raw from his touch and yet she wanted him to go still further, she *loved* feeling like this. And Nikolaos knew it; she was absolutely certain that he knew it. She heard his breathing quicken, felt his powerful body tense, and then he was hard against her, as if he would like to drown himself in her softness and warmth. Desire pulsed between them like a dangerous, uncaged animal, ready to spring, seize, devour. Heat surged through Emily's body, she was giddy, aching, longing for more, terrified of what was going to happen, every nerve utterly raw, but most of all *wanting* —

And he knew exactly how to satisfy that want; his fingers unerringly found the most responsive, the most vulnerable curves and hollows of her body, his mouth could turn a kiss into a turmoil of a hundred different sensations. But his control of his own desire was slipping; he pulled her more tightly against him, the hot closeness bringing both satisfaction and a raging need for even more intimate contact.

Emily found herself shivering in anticipation, closed her eyes as his hand slid beneath the soft cotton of her blouse. Then she stiffened at the sound of a discreet knock on the door, and felt Nikolaos similarly freeze.

'Mr Konstantin,' said his secretary's voice nervously and apologetically, 'there is someone here to see you.'

Nikolaos abruptly drew back, his eyes dark as night. He seemed to get control of himself again very quickly, but it was a few more moments before Emily could even speak.

'I — I'd better go,' she managed to mumble at last.

'Yes, I think that you had,' he said tautly.

Emily ran her fingers through her dishevelled curls, and tried to breathe normally again as she headed rather blindly towards the door. She thought that, at the last moment, Nikolaos might try and stop her leaving, but he didn't. She supposed that he, too, had realised just how close the situation had come to running completely out of control. And from his silence now she guessed that he didn't like it; such a lack of control was something entirely new to him.

As Emily went through to the outer office, where Nikolaos's secretary worked, she was brought to a halt with an abrupt jolt because it was Nikolaos's cousin Sofia who was waiting for him.

Sofia looked exquisite this morning, in a beautifully cut pale cream suit and high-heeled, thin-strapped shoes. Every strand of her glossy black hair was set perfectly into place, and she wore just enough make-up to enhance her dark, vivid features.

By contrast, Emily still felt hot and extremely flustered after those devastating kisses. She also knew from the heat in her cheeks that there was a flush of hectic colour in her face, could feel that her mouth was swollen and bruised, and suspected that her eyes were far too bright.

Sofia's dark gaze slid over Emily, and seemed to take in every dishevelled detail.

'I thought that you would be working, not spending your time in Nikolaos's office,' she said at last, in an extremely cool voice.

'I—we—there were some things we had to discuss,' Emily said rather incoherently.

Sofia looked as if she knew exactly what those things had been. And didn't like it one little bit. To Emily's relief, though, the door to Nikolaos's office opened again at that moment, and Nikolaos himself came out.

'Emily, I——' he began in an edged voice. Then he saw Sofia, and his face changed; he gave his cousin a warm smile.

'We have a lunch date,' Sofia reminded him, walking over and laying one hand possessively on his arm.

'So we do,' he said, standing very close to his beautiful cousin.

'Was there something you wanted to say to Emily?' Sofia asked, rather pointedly.

'Nothing important,' he said smoothly.

Emily took the hint and scuttled out of the office. She was deeply alarmed at the jealousy that had rushed through her as she had seen Nikolaos and Sofia together. Stupid, of course, because it shouldn't matter to her *who* he took to lunch, or spent his spare time with—or even slept with.

An involuntary shiver ran down Emily's spine as she briefly thought of him in bed with the beautiful Sofia. It had probably happened, though. Nikolaos might have a very cynical attitude towards love, but he was still a highly sensual man. She staunchly shook her head and told herself not to think about it; he could sleep with whomever he liked, and it was absolutely nothing to do with her.

She worked furiously hard for the rest of the day. The last twenty-four hours had been extremely disturbing in all different sorts of ways, but she knew that she was going to drive herself a little crazy if she couldn't stop thinking about them. She forced herself to concentrate only on the job in hand. Towards the end of her shift, she was beginning to congratulate herself on having succeeded. She was exhausted, but that was not surprising, since she had probably done the work of three people. She hadn't thought of Nikolaos for—oh, nearly half an hour, she told herself with a sense of accomplishment.

Then one of the bellboys came with a message for her. Nikolaos wanted to see her in the hotel lobby as soon as was convenient.

Emily's new-found composure instantly vanished. She found herself rushing to the nearest mirror, to see if her mane of gold curls had got completely out of hand while she had been working. Then she was immediately furious with herself for behaving like that. She forced herself to march away from the mirror, although she couldn't resist one last glance, to check that she hadn't gone completely white with nerves.

Of course, there was no *reason* to be nervous, she told herself as she made her way down to the lobby. It was just some small item about the running of the hotel that he wanted to discuss with her; he couldn't possibly have any other reason for wanting to see her.

When she got there, she found that the lobby was fairly crowded, and realised at once that that was why he had chosen it for this meeting. With so many people around, there would be absolutely no chance of the situation between them getting out of control again.

All the same, Emily's pulses were thumping uncomfortably hard as she walked towards Nikolaos. And when his black gaze swung round to fix on her, when she saw the familiar planes of his face, the hard line of his mouth, her legs very nearly crumpled completely.

With an effort, she took the last few steps that brought her to his side.

'You wanted to see me?' she said, amazed at how steady her voice sounded, because inside she was a quivering mass of nerves.

'Yes,' he said shortly. 'What happened earlier was —

unfortunate. If we are going to continue working together, then we need to make sure that nothing like it happens again.'

'That's fine with me,' she lied. 'I've never had this sort of problem with an employer before, and I'll be very happy if I don't have it again.'

'I'm not your employer, in the strict sense of the word,' Nikolaos reminded her. 'You're simply working with me to gain experience. You're also free to leave at any time you wish.'

Was that what this was about? Emily thought with new indignation. He was hoping she would just meekly go, and solve the problem?

'I'm not going anywhere,' she said firmly.

'In that case, it must be clearly understood that, in future, our relationship must remain on a strictly business level.'

'I agree with that,' she said with as much bravado as she could muster. 'Is that all you wanted to see me about?'

Nikolaos paused for only a fraction of a second. 'Yes,' he then said, in an unequivocal tone.

Emily quickly left the lobby, and headed up to her room. Her shift was over now, and she was so emotionally and physically drained that she simply wanted to tumble into bed and sleep for several hours.

Halfway up the stairs, though, she suddenly stopped. She had just remembered that lunch date Nikolaos had had with Sofia. Had that had anything to do with that pronouncement from Nikolaos just now? Sofia had seen that hectic flush on Emily's face earlier, and had probably guessed why it was there. Had she then given Nikolaos an ultimatum?

Probably not, Emily decided. Nikolaos wasn't the kind of man who would react well to an ultimatum of any kind, and since Sofia had known him for a very long time she would certainly appreciate that. But she might have made it very clear that he couldn't have her *and* his little cousin from England.

Emily gave a small sigh. And it looked as if Nikolaos had made his choice. Of course, there had never really been any competition.

She tried hard to convince herself that it didn't matter, she didn't — couldn't possibly — want Nikolaos for herself.

Want Nikolaos — the words echoed through her head as she continued much more slowly up the stairs. It was really alarming how hard it was to get rid of that haunting phrase, now that it had lodged itself inside her mind.

CHAPTER SIX

FOR the next couple of days, Emily threw herself into her work with almost frantic intensity. She kept telling herself over and over that she had forgotten all about that silly business with Nikolaos; that there were far more important things that should be occupying her mind. If anyone had asked her what those important things were, she might have had a problem telling them, but she conveniently ignored that fact.

At the end of the week, a message came from Nikolaos's secretary. He was at a business meeting all morning, but would she join him for lunch at a restaurant near the hotel?

Emily immediately ran up to her room and began frenziedly sorting through her wardrobe. Clothes were tried on and then discarded, and her eyes became a little feverish as she couldn't find anything that was quite right.

Then she suddenly stopped and stood quite still. What was she *doing*? This was a simple lunch, not a date. Calming herself down, she picked out a plain skirt and a short sleeved, cool silk blouse. She left her hair loose — there simply wasn't time for any sophisticated styling — but clipped the unruly gold curls back from her face with wide combs. Then she took a couple of very deep breaths and left the hotel.

The restaurant was situated on the promenade. The trees opposite swayed softly in the gentle breeze that blew from the calm blue sea, the air was fresh and clean, and the sun was a warm caress. Boats glided over the barely ruffled water, either heading for the old harbour or setting off on their different voyages, but Emily barely noticed them. Her eyes were already fixed on Nikolaos, who sat at a table set outside the restaurant, obviously waiting for her.

She felt horribly tense, although she was already quite sure that nothing personal was going to be discussed during this lunch. He had chosen once again to meet her in a very public place, and she had the feeling that all their future meetings were going to take place in similar circumstances.

As she sat down opposite him, he handed her the menu.

'What would you like to order?' he asked crisply.

Emily's appetite had disappeared completely, but she forced herself to look at the menu and finally chose *avgolemono*, a lemon-flavoured chicken broth served with rice. Nikolaos ordered *papoutsakia*, aubergine stuffed with minced meat and tomatoes, and topped with beaten egg and breadcrumbs.

When Emily's food arrived, it looked and smelt delicious, but she could only manage a few mouthfuls. She was still nervously waiting to hear why she had been invited to this lunch.

She didn't have to wait for long. Nikolaos finished eating, then looked directly at her, his black eyes very cool, as if he had never touched her, never kissed her, never come so very close to losing all control.

'The main tourist season is now getting under way,' he said without preamble. 'I think that it's time I moved you to Paphos, so that you can take over the running of Dimitri's hotel there.'

Emily blinked. 'Run the hotel? You mean—I'd be completely in charge?'

'Under my supervision, of course.'

'But I didn't think—well, I thought it would be a long time before I'd be ready for a big step like that.'

'You're *not* ready,' Nikolaos told her. 'It takes years, not months, to make a good hotel manager. There are a hundred and one things that you don't yet know, but the best way to learn them is by actually doing the job. I've decided that we'll give it a month's trial. By the end of that time, I'll know whether you'll eventually be capable of dealing on your own with that kind of responsibility.'

'I will be,' Emily assured him. All the same, it was rather awesome to think of being given so much responsibility. And Nikolaos would be there all the time, watching everything she did. They would be working together, spending long hours in each other's company. . .

Emily gave a small gulp. 'It must be very inconvenient for you, having to spend so much time away from your own work. You don't usually spend the summer in Paphos, do you?'

'No,' he agreed, 'but it's no hardship for me to spend the next few weeks there. I've several business interests in the area, and I'm involved in a new hotel and leisure complex that's being built a little further along the coast. I'll easily be able to combine my business affairs with your supervision.'

Emily tried to comfort herself with the thought that they had already agreed that, in future, they would have a strictly working relationship. That should have made her feel more relaxed—safer—but, for some reason, it didn't.

'When do we leave for Paphos?' she asked.

'At the beginning of next week.' A lightly mocking gleam lit his eyes. 'I thought that I should give you plenty of time to pack, considering the amount of luggage that you brought with you.'

Emily nearly blurted out the reason why she had bought all those clothes: the depression that had swept her into that wild shopping spree. At the last moment, though, she stopped herself. Was there any reason to think that Nikolaos would understand — or even believe her?

'I think that my clothes are my affair,' she said rather stiffly.

His black gaze fixed on her. 'You must be counting the days until you can collect your inheritance. Fill your wardrobe with the latest designer labels.'

It *hurt* that he could still have such a low opinion of her; still think that money was the most important thing in her life. She was determined not to let him see how he could get to her, though.

'Of course,' she said in a bright, brittle voice. 'That's why I'm doing all of this, isn't it? So that I can collect my inheritance?'

Nikolaos's face darkened. Then he rather abruptly got to his feet. 'I've an appointment to keep.'

Emily also stood up. 'Then please don't let me keep you. I've also got a lot of work to get on with.'

He growled something under his breath that she couldn't quite hear, then swung round and strode off.

Emily immediately sat down again because her knees were definitely knocking. These confrontations with Nikolaos were getting harder and harder to handle. And she had months of them to endure yet, before the year was up!

On the other hand, she found that she was looking forward to going to Paphos. For one thing, she would see Dimitri's hotel for the first time. She had deliberately not made a special trip to see it before now, because she had wanted to wait until she could walk through the door as the manager.

That was going to happen a lot sooner than she had expected. Of course, it would be under Nikolaos's supervision, but she still felt a tremendous sense of achievement.

She and Nikolaos left for Paphos the following Monday, in Nikolaos's car. She felt both apprehensive and excited as they drove away from Limassol. Her life had changed so dramatically over the last couple of months: here she was on her way to run a large hotel on Cyprus instead of sitting behind her desk in an accountant's office in London, adding up columns of figures and giving advice to clients. Emily had to admit, though, that this was a lot more exciting, and challenging.

Nikolaos glanced at her briefly. 'When we reach the hotel, I suggest that you spend the first few days simply getting to know the staff, going through the account books, and getting yourself accustomed to the way the hotel is run. Don't try and do too much, too soon.'

'But I wanted to get down to some real work straight away,' Emily said at once. 'And I already *know* how a hotel is run.'

'Each hotel is slightly different. You have to get the feel of its character, or things will start to go wrong right from the beginning.'

'I thought that you were going to let me do things my own way?' she said with a small frown. 'That I was going to be given a chance to show what I can really do? But you're already giving me orders!'

Nikolaos's own gaze briefly darkened. 'This hotel meant a great deal to Dimitri. I don't intend to see it ruined through your inexperience or incompetence.'

Emily took a deep breath, ready to argue with him,

but then stopped. She supposed that, annoyingly, he
was right. She *was* inexperienced; it made sense to take
this one step at a time and accept whatever advice was
given her. There was so much she still had to learn
and she really did want to make a success of this.

They reached Paphos just before lunchtime, and she
was enchanted by her first impressions. Brightly coloured boats ringed Paphos's harbour, which was still
guarded at the far end by a medieval fortress. The
water in the sheltered harbour glittered as tiny waves
ruffled its surface, and the boats bobbed very gently, as
if quite content to stay at their moorings instead of
facing the open sea. Tourists chatted and ate in the
warm sun at the tables set out on the quayside, a white
pelican waddled around looking completely at home
and the atmosphere seemed very relaxed and cheerful.

Shortly afterwards, Nikolaos brought the car to a
halt outside a large and very imposing hotel.

'Is this it?' Emily asked, looking up at it slightly
awestruck. 'Dimitri's hotel?'

'The Hotel Konstantin. It has a five-star rating, which
I intend it should keep, so don't even think about
making any major changes without first referring to
me.'

His attitude made Emily bristle again. 'When the
year is up, this hotel will *belong* to me,' she reminded
him indignantly. 'Then I can do whatever I like with
it!'

'But, in the meantime, you will do what *I* tell you,'
Nikolaos said, his dark gaze locking on to hers and
holding it.

Emily was the first one to look away. It was amazing
how intimidating this man's gaze could be.

She was too excited to feel intimidated for long
though. She jumped out of the car and headed towards

the hotel entrance, wanting to explore every room and every corner of the extensive grounds. Her eyes opened wide as she went into the large and rather grand lobby, with its high ceiling, beautifully tiled floor, and long windows that opened on to panoramic views of the sea.

Nikolaos followed more slowly. He spoke briefly to several people as he passed through the lobby, and Emily realised that the staff were beginning to look at her with a mixture of interest and wariness. Nikolaos must have warned them that she would be coming, and they must have been wondering what to expect. She knew that her youth and inexperience would count against her, and that she would have to work hard to win their respect. On the other hand, she was full of enthusiasm, and already had half a dozen half-formed plans for the future whirling round inside her head.

Too excited to eat, she spent the rest of the day wandering around the hotel, familiarising herself with the layout. And there was a lot of it to see! The hotel had two restaurants, a cocktail bar, a small shopping arcade, an outdoor and indoor swimming-pool, a gymnasium, squash and tennis courts, a sauna and a jacuzzi. There was a hairdressing salon and beauty parlour for guests who needed instant glamour, a coffee shop for mid-morning and mid-afternoon breaks, sun terraces that were set among tumbling cascades of flowers that scented the air and small trees that offered welcome patches of shade. Gardens led down to the beach, where the blue waters of the Mediterranean gently lapped against the sand.

Emily was thrilled by everything that she saw; she knew that managing a hotel like this would be the biggest challenge she was every likely to tackle. By the end of the day, though, she was rather overwhelmed by it all, and knew that she needed to get away for just a short while; needed a little time to get used to the idea that, in less than a year, she would be in sole charge of this beautiful hotel.

With a small sense of shock, Emily realised that she had completely abandoned the plans she had once had for going back to England at the end of the year, and continuing her training as an accountant. Even though the past couple of months had had some highly uncomfortable moments—and most of them had been connected in some way with Nikolaos!—she adored it here on Cyprus; every day she felt more at home on this beautiful island. The people were so friendly, everyone seemed very relaxed—except, again, for Nikolaos. And the sun, the warmth, the fresh tang of the sea air, all seemed to suit her down to the ground. She had started to come alive again since arriving here. When she looked in the mirror now, she could see a new glow to her skin, an extra brightness in her vivid blue eyes, her hair seemed to curl more riotously than ever and it shone like spun gold in the bright sunlight.

Emily left the hotel and slowly walked down towards the harbour. The sun was slowly setting, turning the sky a brilliant scorched orange. The squat shape of the medieval castle stood out as a dark silhouette against the dazzling display of the sunset, and the colours of the boats became more muted, drowned by the great glow that lit the sky. Emily gave a wry and slightly sad smile. This was the stuff that romance was made of; there should have been lovers walking off into that sunset. Then her heart seemed to turn right over as she realised that Nikolaos had just fallen into step beside her.

'What—what are you doing here?' she stammered.

'I haven't had dinner yet, and I don't like to eat

alone,' he said casually. 'You don't mind if I join you, do you?'

'N-no,' she said, wishing fervently that her nervously stuttering tongue would behave itself.

They walked on in silence until they reached a taverna on the waterfront, and Emily gradually forced herself to relax a little. She knew that she was going to *have* to relax if she was ever going to get through these last few months working with Nikolaos. She couldn't go through them in a permanent state of nervous tension!

At the taverna, they had a simple meal of *souvlakia*, pieces of lamb marinated in lemon juice, cooked on a spit with chunks of tomatoes, onions and green peppers, and served with pitta bread. By the time they had finished eating, night had fallen, stars were shining in the dark velvet sky, and the sea was flecked with small sparks of silver where it reflected the moonlight.

Nikolaos ordered coffee, to finish their meal, and then sat back and looked at her.

'Now that you've seen the hotel, are you intimidated by the sheer size of it?' he challenged her softly.

'Certainly not,' she said at once, although not altogether truthfully.

'You do understand what you're taking on? You'll be working practically every hour of the day and night, you'll be expected to make endless decisions, you'll have to tackle problems that will range from a small query over a bill to a major crisis. You'll be responsible for every single thing that happens in that hotel, and if anything goes wrong the blame will immediately be put on to you. You'll be expected to maintain the very high standards that give the hotel its five-star rating, and also ensure that the hotel stays profitable. That isn't always as easy as it sounds; tourists come and go, and a resort that's fashionable one year can be out of favour the next.'

'I bet that you think I can't do *any* of those things,' Emily said, her blue eyes flashing indignantly.

'To the contrary,' he replied, to her astonishment. 'I'm beginning to think that, perhaps, you can.'

She blinked in pure disbelief. '*What* did you just say?' she demanded, sure that she must have misheard him.

Nikolaos was silent for a while before finally replying. 'You've turned out to be very different from what I expected. You've a lot more character and determination, you're not afraid of hard work, and you're ready to learn whatever needs to be learnt. And people like you. I watched you working with the staff at my hotel; you got on well with all of them. Your only problem might be that you're sometimes too soft. You can be hurt if people are rude to you, or abuse you. And that will happen,' he warned. 'Remember the problem that you had with Ron Carson, the drunken guest in Limassol. Every hotel has its quota of difficult or downright unpleasant guests. They're a very small minority, but they are something that you'll have to cope with.'

'I'll deal with them,' Emily said staunchly. 'Just watch me!'

'Yes, I think that I will,' Nikolaos said in an unexpectedly soft voice. 'I think that watching you over the next few weeks is going to be very interesting.'

With that, he paid the bill then got up. He turned to go, then swung back and shot her a quick, dark, intense look that made Emily's skin abruptly prickle, despite the gentle warmth of the evening. Then he strode away, and she found that she was biting her lip painfully hard as she watched him disappear from sight.

Slowly, she let her gaze return to the tables that were set outside the taverna. It was only then she realised that someone else seemed to have been watching Nikolaos walk away. A dark figure, almost hidden in the shadows, sitting just outside the pool of light that spilled out from the taverna. Emily could just make out the pale shape of a face that appeared to be staring intently after Nikolaos. Then the pale face turned in her direction, and Emily felt herself come under the same keen scrutiny.

She shifted uncomfortably in her chair. Why was this person so interested in her and Nikolaos?

Emily decided that there was one way to find out. She would go over and ask. She didn't stop to think if that was a wise thing to do, she simply got to her feet and began to walk over. The person at the other table swiftly jumped up, turned round and hurried away. There was time, though, for Emily to see that it was a woman. She had black hair, and was wearing dark jeans and a black shirt, as if she had come here tonight with the intention of blending into the shadows and remaining unseen.

Emily didn't run after her. For one thing, it had been a long day and she was too tired. And for another, the woman had quickly disappeared into the crowds of tourists and locals who had come down to the waterfront for the evening, either for a meal or simply to enjoy the atmosphere of the harbour at night.

Her pale brows drew together again in a puzzled frown. Who was the woman? An old girlfriend of Nikolaos's who had suddenly spotted him, and been rather stunned by his unexpected appearance? She supposed that was an explanation that made sense. Emily could quite understand how the sight of Nikolaos could knock your entire nervous system completely off balance!

During the couple of weeks that followed, Emily didn't have time to think any more about the mystery woman who had watched her and Nikolaos on the quayside. She had thought that she had worked hard at Nikoloas's hotel in Limassol, but that had been nothing compared to the hours she now put in.

She followed Nikolaos's advice, and spent the first few days simply getting to know the staff, the routine of the hotel, and studying its financial structure. Because of the size of the hotel, and the number of staff it employed, that in itself was exhausting. Emily tackled the task steadily, though, making time to talk to everyone, from the girls who cleaned the rooms to the under-managers who were in charge of the different functions of the hotel.

Emily had known from the very start that she would have to move with tact and care. Some of the older and more experienced staff would find it very easy to resent her, stepping straight into the top job. And the younger staff might not want to take orders from someone who was no older than they were. It was much less of a problem that she had expected, though. The smooth and highly efficient running of the hotel was due almost entirely to the attitude of its staff. They worked together with a friendly, easy cheerfulness, and Emily found everyone amazingly helpful as she fumbled her way around during those first few days. And, of course, Nikolaos was there to give advice when it was needed and guide her through all the problems she encountered.

She found that understanding the financial structure was an enormous help. By going through the accounts, she could see at once which areas of the hotel were the most profitable, where there was room for improvement, and how all the different segments fitted together to form a very profitable whole.

By the end of the first couple of weeks, she was exhausted, but confident that she knew how the hotel was run, its character, and the general attitude of its staff. She was ready to tackle the really difficult part now—actually taking over the overall responsibility for the running of the hotel, and trying out one or two of the ideas that she had already had to improve it still further.

On the Monday morning, though, when she was ready to begin, Nikolaos walked into her office unannounced and sat on the edge of her desk.

His dark eyes fixed on her face, and then he gave a small frown. 'You look as if you haven't slept for several days.'

'I've been very busy,' she said pointedly.

'Too busy. I didn't expect you to try and learn absolutely everything in these first couple of weeks.'

'Did you think I'd just sit back and let the hotel run itself while I lazed around in the sun all day?'

'No, but it's possible to go to the other extreme. You need a break.' He thought for a few moments. 'I'm going to visit my aunt this afternoon,' he said at last. 'You can come with me.'

Emily looked at him in astonishment. 'But I thought that none of your family wanted to meet me?'

'There has been some—curiosity expressed about you,' Nikolaos said drily. 'Perhaps it's time that you finally met one or two of your relatives.'

'They're not my relatives.' Emily reminded him. 'I'm not a Konstantin, I didn't even change my surname when Dimitri married my mother.'

'You're still connected to the Konstantins by marriage. That makes you part of the family.'

To her surprise, Emily found that she liked the idea of belonging to a family. She had so few relatives of her own, it would be nice to be able to add to them.

Then she gave a reluctant shake of her head. 'I can't possibly go and visit your aunt, I'm far too busy.'

'No, you're not,' Nikolaos said calmly. 'I'm ordering you to take the afternoon off. That still gives you the rest of the morning to deal with anything urgent, and get yourself ready.'

'I really can't go,' Emily said again, although with far less conviction this time. She knew very well that she was dying to take up this very unexpected invitation to visit Nikolaos's aunt. So far, apart from Nikolaos, the only other Konstantin she had met was Sofia, and that hadn't been a riotous success! But, with luck, his aunt would be a true Cypriot, friendly and talkative — and a mine of information. Emily was beginning to realise that there were a great many things she was itching to know about the Konstantins — and, in particular, about Nikolaos.

'I'll pick you up at one o'clock,' Nikolaos told her firmly. 'Make sure you're ready on time.'

For once, Emily was glad that he had overridden her arguments. Nikolaos was right, she did need a break from work. And she simply couldn't resist this opportunity to meet one of his family.

She whizzed through the morning's work, gulped down a sandwich and some coffee, and then rushed to get ready. After a moment's thought, she put on a plain white blouse, a navy skirt, and a pair of flat shoes. She forced her thickly curling hair under control with the help of a couple of large slides. Then she went down to meet Nikolaos.

When he saw her coming towards him, his eyebrows drew together in a distinct frown. 'You look like a schoolgirl,' he commented, obviously not pleased by her appearance. 'Why are you dressed like that?'

'I thought that your aunt might be elderly. And rather conventional. I wanted to look—well, respectable,' she admitted sheepishly.

Nikolaos gave an unexpected smile, which completely changed his face. 'My aunt isn't elderly and she certainly isn't conventional. We've a few minutes to spare. Go and put something on that makes you look older than sixteen! I don't want everyone to look at me disapprovingly because they think I'm trying to seduce someone half my age.'

Emily felt herself go bright red, wasn't sure *why* she had gone that embarrassing colour, but thought it might have something to do with the fact that the prospect of being seduced by Nikolaos did the oddest things to her entire nervous system. She mumbled something under her breath, hurriedly turned round and rushed back to her room.

Ten minutes later, she reappeared in a short skirt that clung to her slender hips, a loose top that barely disguised the fact that she had unexpectedly full breasts for a slim girl, and high-heeled sandals that showed off her lightly tanned legs to stunning advantage. Her golden hair, released from the slides, fell in its usual riot of untamed curls around her face, and she had used just the minimum of make-up to emphasise her long lashes, the vivid blue of her eyes and the generous line of her mouth.

For just a moment, Nikolaos seemed startled by the transformation. His dark eyes briefly glowed and the hard line of his mouth relaxed into a more sensual outline. Then he was quickly in control of himself again.

'Let's get going,' he said briefly. 'I don't want to be late.'

Sitting beside him in the car, Emily asked, 'Where does your aunt live?'

'A few kilometres north of here, in my villa at Coral Bay.'

'You've got a villa?' she said, surprised.

'Do you think that I live in hotels all the time?' he said drily.

'No—I suppose not—well, I've never actually thought about it,' she confessed.

'I've also got a house in the Troodos mountains, and apartments in Limassol, Nicosia, London and Paris.'

'That's a lot of houses and apartments to stand empty when you're not using them,' she said slightly disapprovingly.

'Oh, they're rarely empty,' Nikolaos said in a wry tone. 'Some member of my family always manages to move in as soon as I move out. My aunt's staying at my villa, as I've already told you, two cousins are using my apartment in Nicosia, another aunt is staying at the Limassol apartment while her house is being redecorated, and both the London and Paris flats are being used by younger members of the family who are spending a few months abroad, supposedly to study languages.'

'And your house in the Troodos mountains?'

Nikolaos didn't answer straight away, this time. 'My father is living there,' he said at last, in a very different tone of voice.

Emily could tell from his sudden change of mood that she had accidentally strayed on to dangerous ground. She also realised that he never spoke about his father, which was surprising since his family was obviously very important to him. She wanted to ask more questions, but stopped herself. There was obviously some kind of problem between Nikolaos and his father, and it wasn't her business to try and find out what it was.

It didn't take them long to reach Coral Bay. Low hills shimmered in the distance, and the bay itself was surrounded by white cliffs, with pinkish sand sloping down to the clear blue sea. Since it wasn't yet the height of the tourist season, the beach wasn't over-crowded, and the great sweep of the bay meant that there was plenty of room for everyone.

Nikolaos's villa was a long, elegant white building perched on the very edge of the cliff, its great arched windows looking over the bay, right out to sea. Emily wished that they could stay until early evening, so that she could sit at those windows and watch one of the spectacular sunsets for which this coast was famous.

Inside the villa, it felt pleasantly cool, in contrast to the hot, bright sun that shone down outside. She was glad of that. Any time spent with Nikolaos seemed to leave her feeling distinctly flushed!

Nikolaos led her through to a large room at the back of the villa, which had stunning views of the bay. Emily was rather more interested in the rather plump, smiling woman sitting beside one of the windows, though.

'Aunt Anna, this is Emily Peterson, Dimitri's step-daughter,' Nikolaos said formally. 'Emily, this is my aunt Anna.'

'*Kalimera,*' Emily said a little shyly. '*Pos iste?*'

'*Kala, efkharisto, ke sis?*'

'Yes, I'm also well,' Emily replied, still in Greek.

'We were all so very sorry to hear about Dimitri; he

was much loved. You must miss him very much. But it's nice that you could come here to Cyprus, his home.'

'*Efkharisto*——' began Emily, but Nikolaos interrupted a little abruptly.

'Emily, there's no need to struggle along in Greek. My aunt speaks excellent English.'

'Emily isn't struggling,' said his aunt at once. 'Her Greek is very good. And I think that she could give you a few lessons in politeness, Nikolaos.'

'Emily has already given me lessons in quite a few things,' he said in a more resigned voice. 'Is your ankle better, Aunt Anna?'

She lifted up her brightly coloured skirt to show a surprisingly well shaped ankle. 'The swelling has almost gone,' she said with some satisfaction. 'I walked down to the beach and back this morning.'

Emily blinked, because she could see the path down to the beach from the window. It was very steep, and even someone with two perfectly good ankles would have to go very carefully.

'How did you hurt your ankle?' she asked Nikolaos's aunt.

Nikolaos answered for her. 'My aunt decided that she wanted to learn to water ski,' he said drily.

This time, Emily's eyes nearly popped out as she tried—and failed!—to imagine this plump, middle-aged woman on water skis.

'The first few lessons went very well,' Aunt Anna said indignantly. 'The accident really wasn't my fault. There was a bow-wave from a boat that came much too close, and I didn't see it until it was too late—I won't make the same mistake again next time,' she said confidently.

'You're going to carry on with the lessons?' Emily said in growing admiration.

'Of course,' she said without hesitation. 'Everyone should try something new now and then. If you don't, you just get old and boring.'

'I'm sure that no one's ever considered you boring,' Nikolaos said, his dark eyebrows gently raised.

'And they never will,' said his aunt, with some determination. 'I'm going to windsurf next year. I've sat at this window and watched people doing it in the bay, and it looks great fun. Can you windsurf?' she asked Emily.

'Er — no,' Emily admitted. 'But I've always wanted to have a go.'

'We could learn together,' suggested his aunt.

'I'd really like that. I've been here for nearly three months now, but there's still so much that I haven't done or seen.'

'Nikolaos, you must organise some breaks for both yourself and Emily. And you must take some time off and show her around the island,' Aunt Anna ordered.

'Yes, Aunt Anna,' Nikolaos said with some resignation, as if he was used to receiving orders from his aunt. Then he glanced at his watch. 'I've some phone calls to make. Do you mind if I leave the two of you for half an hour?'

'Of course not,' said his aunt. 'It will give me a chance to talk to Emily.'

Nikolaos left the room, and Aunt Anna spent the next quarter of an hour skilfully finding out a great deal about Emily. Her questions were put in such a way, though, that Emily found she didn't mind answering them. Eventually, she gave a wry grin.

'You must know just about everything about me by now. Why are you so interested?'

'Because this is the first time Nikolaos has ever

brought a woman here to his house. Except for Sofia, of course.'

Emily gave a small shrug. 'Perhaps he likes to keep his home life private.'

'Nikolaos likes to keep *everything* private,' said his aunt, with a small sigh. Then her eyes brightened again. 'But don't you understand what I am saying? On Cyprus, it is very significant when a man brings a woman to his home like this.'

'Oh, no,' Emily said at once, her heart suddenly thumping, 'you're wrong. It isn't significant at all. He only brought me because he thought I'd been working too hard and needed a break.'

Aunt Anna looked disappointed. 'Are you sure? Only a woman who is very special would be invited here to his house, and brought to meet me, his closest relative apart from his mother and father.'

But Emily refused to believe that Nikolaos's invitation to come here had been anything except casual. 'There's no significance behind it,' she repeated firmly. Then, wanting to change the subject rather quickly, she went on, 'How exactly are you related to Nikolaos?'

'His mother is my sister,' replied Aunt Anna.

'*Is* your sister?' Emily said in surprise. 'But I thought—I mean, no one actually said so, but I assumed——'

'Assumed what?' asked his aunt.

'Well—that his mother was dead,' she said awkwardly.

Aunt Anna immediately looked doleful. 'Nikolaos behaves as if she is dead. It's a very sad story. And it was a great scandal in the family, of course.'

'I know about Dimitri breaking his engagement to Nikolaos's mother. And that she married Dimitri's brother on the rebound, and it didn't work out.'

'No, it didn't,' agreed his aunt. 'But some years later Nikolaos's mother *did* fall in love again. It was with an American, who was here on holiday. It was one of these "love at first sight" affairs. And when he left to go back to America Eléni — Nikolaos's mother — went with him.'

'She ran off?' said Emily, her eyes opening very wide because she knew how sacrosanct the family was on Cyprus. 'She left her husband and her son?'

Aunt Anna nodded sadly. 'Nikolaos was twelve at the time, not a child but not a man. It's a very difficult age, when you feel things intensely. He never forgave his mother, refused to have any contact with her. He destroyed the letters she sent, wouldn't speak to her on the phone. Even today, he won't even mention her name. And his father — ' Aunt Anna sighed heavily. 'His father has never been the same since Eléni left. That is another reason why Nikolaos feels so bitterly towards his mother.'

'And why he's so cynical about love,' said Emily almost to herself. 'He's seen how destructive it can be when it runs out of control.'

'But it's also destructive to live without any love at all,' said his aunt, shaking her head.

'But — he's fond of Sofia, isn't he?' Emily asked hesitantly.

Aunt Anna gave a small snort. 'Sofia! She's no good for Nikolaos. She wants him for all the wrong reasons, because of his wealth, his position, his eligibility. I've told Nikolaos again and again that he'll be miserable for the rest of his life if he marries her.'

Emily swallowed very hard. 'And — and will he marry her?' It was extraordinarily difficult to get out that one short question.

'I don't know,' said Aunt Anna gloomily. 'It's always

been understood in the family, ever since they were children, that they would one day marry. But he would be much happier with someone like you,' she went on, her eyes suddenly brightening. 'I think that I will tell him that before he leaves.'

'No—don't,' Emily said in sudden panic. 'I'm not—I mean, I don't want——'

'Of course you do,' his aunt interrupted her. 'I can see it in the way you look at him. But don't worry,' she went on kindly, 'I won't tell him, if you don't want me to. Anyway, this is something that he perhaps needs to find out for himself.'

'What do I need to find out?' asked Nikolaos, walking back into the room.

Emily immediately went a brilliant scarlet, and shot an imploring look at his aunt.

'Nothing important,' said Aunt Anna. Then she reconsidered. 'Yes, it *is* important,' she corrected herself. 'But you are the one who will have to discover just how important it is.'

'My aunt likes riddles,' said Nikolaos drily, turning to Emily. 'Do you have the slightest idea what she's talking about?'

'No, I don't,' she lied, hoping the frantic colour had faded from her face.

Nikolaos looked at her curiously but, to her intense relief, didn't question her further.

They stayed a little longer at the villa, with Nikolaos and his aunt talking together easily but Emily taking very little part in the conversation. And when they finally left she was still slightly flushed and breathing rather unevenly.

She was also in something of a panic. If Aunt Anna could so easily guess her feelings, how long would it be before Nikolaos also noticed? Also, she didn't seem to be very good at keeping things secret from him. What if she just blurted it out? Emily gave a small shudder. She could just imagine what Nikolaos's reaction would be. Or perhaps, even worse, he would simply laugh, think the whole thing an entertaining joke.

But Emily was already learning that there wasn't anything in the least funny about falling in love with Nikolaos Konstantin.

She had come to Aphrodite's island, the island of love, never suspecting that its magic could ever touch *her*. And now that it had she was astonished, oddly exhilarated and completely terrified.

CHAPTER SEVEN

I'M SURE I haven't fallen in love with him, it's just an infatuation; it *can't* be love.

Emily spent half the night feverishly denying something which should have been very obvious to her a long time ago. And when she had given up trying to deny it she tried something else.

All right, I might — like him a lot more than I should, but it isn't going to get me anywhere, so I'd better forget about it.

That worked a little better. She was good at forgetting things. She had forgotten — almost forgotten — the violence that had marred her childhood. Surely she could forget that she had developed a childish infatuation for her cousin, Nikolaos?

Emily gave a small sigh and closed her eyes. It would be so much easier to forget if he had never kissed her, never triggered that hot ache in her body that had since never quite gone away. She told herself that she had to get some sleep. She had a very full workload planned out for tomorrow, and she was never going to get through it if she was asleep on her feet.

She finally managed to doze fitfully for a couple of hours before dawn. She woke up again just as the sun was rising, and padded over to the window on bare feet, heavy-eyed and yawning.

She had chosen a room for herself that looked out over the small harbour at Paphos. Now, as she stood at the window, the early morning light glinted on the water in the harbour, and she could see men already moving around on the fishing boats, checking the nets and equipment. Tables were being set out on the waterfront, ready for anyone who wanted to eat breakfast outside in the warm sunshine. Beyond the harbour, the sea was very calm, and already a startling blue as it reflected the clear azure of the sky. Its surface was rippled only by a couple of passing boats that left thin trails of gold in their wake as their bow-waves caught the first rays of the sun.

Emily felt the tranquillity of the scene slowly relax her frayed nerves. On a sudden impulse, she quickly showered and dressed, then left the hotel and walked down to the harbour.

It was still early, and few tourists were about yet. She sat down at one of the tables and ordered a cup of coffee, then stared rather dreamily out to sea. She finally drank her coffee and reluctantly decided she had to make her way back to the hotel. She had so much work to get through, she couldn't sit here and daydream all day.

She was about to get up when she became aware that someone was looking at her. And looking very intently. Emily half turned her head, to get a better look at the person who was subjecting her to this intense scrutiny, and found herself staring at a dark-haired, middle-aged but still very handsome woman, sitting several tables away.

For some reason, Emily was absolutely certain that it was the same woman who had been staring at her and Nikolaos in this same spot, on the night of her arrival in Paphos. Who *was* she, though? And what did she want?

Emily decided that, this time, she wasn't going to give the woman a chance to run away. She was going to walk straight over and demand to know what was going on.

Before she had the chance to get out of her chair, though, the woman herself got up and walked over to Emily's table.

'May I sit down?' she asked in a low, beautiful voice.

'Yes—yes, of course,' Emily said, wondering what this was all about.

'You're Emily Peterson, aren't you?' asked the woman.

'How do you know my name?' Emily asked suspiciously.

'I asked someone at the hotel. They told me who you were. You're Dimitri's stepdaughter, and you've come here to Paphos to run his hotel.'

By now, Emily was beginning to get a little ruffled. She didn't like the idea of a stranger prying into her private life.

'Why are you interested in me?' she asked with a small frown.

'Because I've seen you a couple of times with—with Nikolaos. And I want—I *need*—you to help me.'

The woman seemed to stumble a little over Nikolaos's name, as if she found it difficult to say it out loud. Emily's heart immediately sank. Her first guess must have been right; this woman, although so much older than Nikolaos, must be an ex-lover. Did she think that Emily was stepping in to take her place? Was there going to be an unpleasant scene?

'Look,' said Emily very firmly, 'I don't know what you want, but I'm sure that I can't help you.'

'But you must,' said the woman with fresh urgency. '*Someone* must help me. I really can't go on like this for very much longer.' Then, to Emily's alarm, she began to cry, not making a sound, but just letting great tears roll silently down her face.

Emily hurriedly fished a clean handkerchief out of her pocket and offered it to the woman. She wiped dry her big, beautiful dark eyes, then looked back at Emily.

'I'm sorry—I didn't mean to do that. It's just that I'm desperate to find a way of getting to Nikolaos, and I was hoping so much—that—well, that you would——'

'No,' Emily interrupted, with a small shiver. Right now, she just couldn't cope with one of Nikolaos's ex-lovers. 'No, I can't—I *won't* do it. If you want to see Nikolaos, it's perfectly simple. Just go to the hotel and ask to make an appointment with him.'

'He won't see me,' said the woman in a dull voice.

'Then I'm sorry, but I honestly don't see what I can do.'

'Talk to him,' she said with fresh intensity. 'I've seen you together, and I could see just from watching you that you were close to him. Try and persuade him to see me, even if it's just for a few minutes.'

'I can't interfere in his personal life,' Emily said a little helplessly, wishing that this woman would just go away, leave her alone. 'He hates that. If you've had some kind of quarrel with him, if you want to try and get together again, then you'll really have to do it yourself.'

'Oh, God, who do you think I am?' said the woman despairingly. 'An old girlfriend? I'm Eléni Stanton. I used to be Eléni Konstantin—I'm Nikolaos's mother!'

Emily just stared at the older woman for a while, totally stunned. 'His—his mother?' she finally managed to get out in a completely shaken voice.

Eléni looked directly at her with dark eyes that Emily now realised were unnervingly like her son's. 'You do

know about me, don't you? You know that I walked
out on Nikolaos and his father nearly twenty years
ago?'

'Yes,' Emily said in a very low voice. Then she said
in a sudden rush, 'How could you do something like
that?'

'I didn't have any choice,' Eléni said simply. 'I met
Alex, I fell in love, and I was lost. Nothing else
mattered; I was completely obsessed with him, I'd have
given up anything, gone anywhere, just to be with him.
The way I felt about him made the love I'd once felt
for Dimitri seem almost childish, and I knew that I'd
never actually loved my husband at all. I should never
have married him; I made both of us completely
unhappy.'

'But—Nikolaos,' Emily said almost accusingly. 'You
must have loved *him.*'

'Of course I did. He was my only child. I wanted to
take him with me, but Alex wouldn't let me. He said
that it would be bad enough for my husband to lose
me, it would kill him to lose his son as well. Making
the decision to leave Nikolaos behind was the hardest
thing I'd ever done in my life, but I knew that Yannis,
Nikolaos's father, needed him more than I did.' Eléni's
mouth twisted into a painful line. 'I've certainly paid
for that decision over the years,' she said bitterly. 'I
knew that Nikolaos would hate me for a while, but I
always hoped that, once he was an adult himself and
knew what it was like to experience such an overwhelming love for someone, he would understand, perhaps
even forgive me. But he still hates me, still refuses to
have any contact with me.'

'Of course he does,' Emily said almost pityingly.
'Your son *doesn't* know what it's like to love like that;
he's completely cynical about love. He saw it wreck his

own family, he sees it only as a destructive force. He himself only intends to marry because he eventually wants children; he doesn't want a wife he can *love*.' She stopped short there, realising that she had already said far too much.

Eléni had gone very white. 'I didn't know that I had done that to him,' she whispered.

Emily's own heart twisted in sudden sympathy. 'Look,' she said awkwardly, 'I really don't think there's anything I can do. But if I do get a chance to help in any way, then I will. That's really all I can promise you.'

'I'm grateful for that much,' Eléni said quietly. 'And I'm sorry if I've embarrassed you, and made things difficult for you, by talking to you like this. It's just that, when I saw you and Nikolaos together — saw the way he looked at you — '

'He didn't look at me in any special way,' Emily broke in quickly.

Eléni looked at her a little puzzled. 'I'm sure that he did.'

'No, you're wrong,' Emily insisted. She pushed her chair back from the table. 'I've got to get back to work,' she said in a rather flustered voice.

'Please, let me give you my address and phone number,' said Eléni. 'A friend of Alex's is letting me use his holiday home, just outside Paphos.' She scribbled it down on a piece of paper, and held it out to Emily.

After just a moment's hesitation, she took it. Then she looked at Eléni. 'You and Alex,' she said a little awkwardly, 'do you still — feel the same way about each other?'

'Of course,' Eléni said at once. 'Alex is my whole life; I adore him.' She gave the very faintest of smiles.

'And he tells me so often that he loves me that I have to believe him.'

Emily felt a small pang of jealousy. What would it be like, to love someone like that? And be loved so completely in return?

'Then you don't regret giving up so much, to be with him?' she couldn't stop herself from asking, knowing that she shouldn't be asking such personal questions, but longing to know more, because she had no experience of such an intense relationship.

'Of course I have regrets,' Eléni said in a low tone. 'I know that walking out on my family was a terrible thing to do; I won't ever forgive myself for that. But I couldn't stop myself from going. I wanted to have everything, of course, my family and Alex, but I couldn't so, God forgive me, I chose Alex. I know that it was a totally selfish decision, and that I've probably alienated myself from my son forever because of it. Nikolaos is very much a Cypriot at heart — his family means everything to him, and I destroyed the closest part of that family.'

Emily gave a small shiver and hoped that she would never have to make such a choice. 'I'm glad that you came over and spoke to me,' she said at last in a very subdued voice.

'Please get in touch with me if there's any way you can help me to speak to Nikolaos,' Eléni said urgently.

'Yes, I will. I promise.' She stood up. 'I'm afraid that I really do have to go now.' She held her hand out to Eléni, who lightly touched it. Then Emily quickly walked away because she found it hard to look any longer into those dark eyes that were so like Nikolaos's, but softer, more anguished, vulnerable in a way that Nikolaos's could never be.

Emily walked back to the hotel in a daze. This was

the very last thing she had ever expected to happen, to meet Nikolaos's mother. And the sorrow in her eyes! Eléni might have found some kind of happiness with Alex Stanton, her American lover and now her husband, but her decision to walk out on her family had obviously killed part of her. And her continued estrangement from her son was something that she clearly just couldn't bear any longer.

With a soft sigh, Emily acknowledged to herself that there was probably very little she could do to help Eléni. She already knew how implacable Nikolaos could be about certain things, and she was absolutely sure that included his attitude to his mother. Like all Greek men, Nikolaos had a great deal of pride. He would never openly admit how much he had been hurt by all the troubles of the past. And, added to that, he would fiercely protect his family from anything that threatened it, and shun anyone who had hurt it in any way. Even his own mother.

She went through the rest of the day with a troubled face and only half her mind on her work. She felt as if she badly needed someone to speak to, and almost rang Nikolaos's Aunt Anna. She was obviously a kind, understanding woman, and she was also Eléni's sister. Then Emily remembered that Aunt Anna was living in Nikolaos's villa, and was clearly very fond of her nephew. She had obviously chosen which side she wanted to support in this divided family, and might not be at all pleased to learn that Eléni was back on Cyprus. Anyway, if Eléni had thought her sister could help, surely she would have got in touch with her herself?

A couple of times during the afternoon, Emily found herself heading in the direction of Nikolaos's office, determined to confront him with the news that his mother was here, and wanted to see him. Then she would come to an abrupt halt before she even reached his door, afraid of his reaction when he discovered that she was trying to meddle in something that he would consider none of her business. And yet she had promised Eléni. . .

Emily slept fitfully that night, and got up early the next morning full of fresh determination. She *would* speak to Nikolaos; he had to know that his mother was here on Cyprus, desperate to speak to him.

She got as far as the door to his office, then discovered that her legs were beginning to shake. Annoyed at her own cowardice, she forced herself to knock firmly on the door, then marched inside without waiting to be invited.

As soon as Nikolaos's dark gaze fixed on her face, though, she felt the last of her courage simply drain away. He looked so very unapproachable this morning, almost as if he knew why she was here, although she knew that was quite impossible.

'What is it?' he said rather tersely. 'A problem?'

'N-no — well, that is — not really, b-but ——' she stuttered rather incoherently.

He put down his pen. 'Would you like to start again?'

Emily swallowed hard, and knew that she couldn't even say Eléni's name. She just didn't have enough nerve. Instead, she hunted around for some excuse for being here.

'I wanted to talk to you about — about some plans I have for the future,' she said rather lamely, at last.

Nikolaos raised one dark eyebrow. 'And do you find me so terrifying that the prospect of discussing those plans with me has reduced you to a gibbering wreck?'

'I'm *not* gibbering,' Emily said indignantly, conveniently forgetting that she had been doing precisely that a few moments ago.

Nikolaos sat back in his chair. 'Then take a seat,' he invited. 'Tell me about these plans.'

Emily told herself that she would talk to him about his mother soon, *very* soon, but not today. This morning, she really would discuss her plans for the future.

'I've been going through the record of hotel bookings for the past couple of years,' she began, 'and it didn't take me long to realise that we're almost completely booked through the summer, but we still have quite a few vacancies outside the main tourist season.'

Nikolaos nodded. 'That applies to most hotels.'

'I've been trying to think of ways to attract more people here in the slack season,' Emily went on, with growing enthusiasm. 'And I've come up with an idea which I think might work. A lot of people celebrate their wedding anniversaries by taking a holiday, a sort of second honeymoon. Especially if it's a special anniversary, such as a silver or gold. Well, why can't we persuade them to come *here*? After all, Cyprus is the island of love, it's the perfect place for a second honeymoon. I thought we could offer a special package, with extras such a flower-filled room with a romantic view, an anniversary cake, special attention from the staff, and of course trips to all the local places connected with Aphrodite, the goddess of love. We could advertise it as a week of romance, and do everything we can to make their stay here really special.'

'We already organise trips to most of the local places of interest, including those connected with Aphrodite,' Nikolaos pointed out. Then, as Emily's face began to fall, he went on, 'But if you think you can put together an attractive package, by all means try. Get it ready in time, and we'll run it as an experiment next autumn, when the summer bookings begin to tail off.'

'Right,' she said with enthusiasm. 'I've already drawn up a list of the things we can offer here, at the hotel, together with a detailed breakdown of the costs. What I want to do next is visit some of the places connected with the legend of Aphrodite. Her birthplace at Petra tou Romiou, Aphrodite's Baths—oh, and the Fontana Amorosa, of course, the Fountain of Love.'

'The fountain of love is little more than a muddy well,' Nikolaos warned drily.

'Even muddy wells can be romantic, if you're in the right frame of mind,' Emily declared firmly. 'And by the time I've finished with them my guests will definitely be in the mood for love!'

'We'll go tomorrow morning, then.'

'*We'll* go?' she repeated, in surprise.

'Make sure you're ready to leave early,' he said, ignoring her reaction. 'That way, we should avoid the main rush of tourists who'll turn up later.'

'Oh—right—fine,' she said, slightly flustered. She wasn't at all sure that she wanted to visit the legendary haunts of Aphrodite with Nikolaos, of all people, but it didn't look as if she was being given much choice. Anyway, at some time during the day she might be able to find a suitable moment to speak to him about his mother—although Emily couldn't think of *any* moment that would be suitable to discuss such a dangerously personal subject.

She was up before dawn the next morning, and ready to leave by the time the first glimmer of light was showing in the sky. Nikolaos was waiting for her in the lobby, dressed with uncharacteristic informality in jeans and a crisp white shirt that contrasted starkly with his darkly tanned skin and black hair.

As always happened nowadays, the sight of him sent Emily's pulses thumping faster and harder. She fer-

vently hoped that none of her inner turmoil showed on
her face, and made herself breathe slowly and steadily
as she got into the car beside him.

As they drove south-eastwards out of Paphos,
towards the legendary birthplace of Aphrodite, she
shot a couple of quick glances at him. The strong lines
of his face were so very familiar to her by now, and the
casual clothes seemed to emphasise the powerful
muscles of his body. Emily felt a small army of goose-
pimples suddenly march over her skin, and knew very
well that it wasn't because there was still a very faint
chill in the early morning air.

The road ran right along the edge of the coast, so
that Emily could see the first rays of the sun beginning
to glint on the water. The sky was a pale azure now,
but would soon deepen to a richer blue as another hot
and perfect day got under way. A heat haze would
shimmer over the mountains, and the island would
bake lazily in the sun that drenched it.

Nikolaos brought the car to a halt as the road curved
round yet another small bay. 'This is it,' he said.
'Aphrodite's birthplace.'

A narrow path led down to the cove below. At the
head of the cove was a giant rock, surrounded by
several smaller outcrops. The waves broke gently on the
shingle beach, and they were touched by the rising sun,
creating a thin line of foam that shone almost golden in
the early morning light.

Emily got out of the car and walked slowly down to
the beach. Nikolaos followed, and then stood beside
her as she kicked off her sandals and dipped her toes
into the cool water. She turned and softly smiled at
him, seduced by the magic of the legend, a beautiful
woman rising up out of the foam of the sea.

'Do you think that it really happened?' she said a

little dreamily. 'Did Aphrodite really come ashore here and live on this island?'

Nikolaos looked back at her, and Emily wondered if it was the clear light of late dawn that was causing that bright glitter in his eyes.

'Sometimes, it's possible to believe almost anything,' he said rather abruptly. Then he turned away and began to walk back up the beach, leaving Emily with little choice except to follow him.

Back in the car, they retraced the route to Paphos, then turned north, towards Aphrodite's Baths. The sun was getting much warmer now, and Emily was glad that she had chosen to wear just a thin, sleeveless cotton dress. Her hair tumbled down to her shoulders in its usual cascade of golden curls, and the thin gold bracelet that she wore as her only jewellery glinted against the healthy, lightly tanned glow of her skin.

She knew that there was a car park and tourist pavilion near the Baths of Aphrodite, so she was surprised when Nikolaos instead drove into a small fishing village and then stopped the car.

'Why have we come here?' she asked. 'The Baths of Aphrodite are further along the road.'

'You also wanted to see the Fountain of Love, didn't you?'

'Yes, I did.'

'Since the road leading to it isn't suitable for ordinary cars, the easiest way to reach it is by boat.'

'By boat?' Emily echoed, with new interest. 'That's rather romantic; I'm sure people here on a second honeymoon would enjoy that.'

Nikolaos looked sceptical, but said nothing. Emily gave a tiny sigh. She supposed that she should stop talking about love and romance, since Nikolaos clearly wasn't interested in either. She could understand that because, until a few weeks ago, she had known so little about it, hadn't even been particularly interested herself.

Something had happened to her since her arrival on Cyprus, though. Something inside of her had changed — perhaps forever. Emily's nerves gave a gentle quiver, because that was a rather frightening thought. She couldn't run away from it any longer, however. She didn't know *what* had changed her — the warm glow of the sun, the scent of the flowers, the relaxed atmosphere and friendly, easygoing people, or perhaps even the influence of the legendary Aphrodite herself. She just knew that she was opening up, flowering, starting to want things that she had never really wanted before. Or, remembering the violent relationship between her mother and her father, had shied away from. And all these new feelings were tied up with Nikolaos, which was *really* scary, because underneath that formidable façade was a very sensual man. And Emily wasn't so naïve and innocent that she didn't realise that Nikolaos could easily separate love and desire, rejecting one but pursuing the other with a single-minded determination that would be difficult — perhaps impossible — to resist.

Which meant that she should be spending as little time with him as possible, because each day seemed to find her more vulnerable to him. She certainly shouldn't be going on this journey with him to the haunts of Aphrodite, the goddess of love.

Yet Emily didn't make some excuse to return to the hotel. Instead, she followed Nikolaos down to the small harbour at Latchi. And she willingly got into the small boat that was waiting for them.

An older, darkly tanned man, stripped to the waist, grinned at Nikolaos and greeted him. Then he started up the engine and the boat began to move out of the harbour. The sun was brighter now, lighting up the mountains that rose up behind the village, and tipping the small waves with bright sparks of light as the boat picked up speed and left the harbour behind. Nikolaos obviously knew the boat owner, because he asked after various members of his family. Emily lazily sat back and listened to the sound of Nikolaos's voice, deep and confident, quite unlike any other man's voice. At the same time, her gaze roamed over the curve of the coast with its small bays lapped by the blue sea, and the rising swell of the mountains behind it, their pale, sunscorched slopes dappled with the different greens of olive, cypress, fig, carob and almond trees. This morning, the very shape of the island seemed sensual, and she found herself stretching luxuriously, as if some of that sensuality was seeping into her own veins.

The boat chugged slowly to a halt alongside a rocky outcrop. There was no purpose-built landing area; anyone wanting to go ashore simply jumped out on to the rock.

Nikolaos went first, and then held his hand out to Emily. She hesitated for only an instant before letting him catch hold of her with a firm, hard grip. When they were both ashore, the boatman waved to them, and then headed his boat back out to sea. Emily turned to Nikolaos in alarm.

'How do we get back again?'

'We walk,' he said. 'The best way to see this part of the island is on foot. But first I'll show you the Fountain of Love.'

As he had warned, it was no more than a muddy well, but Emily still found it fascinating. And it was so marvellously quiet and peaceful here; the only sound came from the birds which sang tunefully from the trees, and the insects that buzzed around lazily in the growing heat. The main blaze of spring flowers was over now, but butterflies flitted silently among the few late blooms that were left, and a couple of small lizards scuttled, carefully avoiding Emily's feet.

'No wonder Aphrodite chose to live here,' she said dreamily. 'It's so beautiful.'

'Aphrodite didn't exist,' Nikolaos reminded her. 'Except in people's imaginations.'

'Well, my imagination is working overtime at the moment,' she said in the same dreamy voice. 'I can almost see her, drifting through the trees, on her way to meet one of her lovers ——'

'You sound as if you wish *you* were on your way to meet a lover,' Nikolaos said softly.

Something in his tone of voice brought her abruptly back to reality. 'No, of course I don't,' she said, much more sharply than she had intended. It was a lie, though. Emily was beginning to long for love; she wasn't frightened of it any more. The memories of the violent relationship between her mother and her father seemed to be fading a little with every day that she spent on this beautiful, peaceful island. And, without even knowing that he had done it, Nikolaos had taught her that men could be physically powerful, and yet still be capable of gentleness, when it was needed. That they could lose their tempers, and yet not resort to violence, not lash out indiscriminately and hurt whoever was nearest to them. That desire could be controlled, and the restless energy that it generated channelled into work and concern for the family, instead of becoming pent-up and destructive.

But he had also taught her what it was like to *want* someone. That was probably the most dangerous lesson she had ever learned, and one of the most painful. She knew that it was useless to want Nikolaos; he wasn't interested in what she could offer him. If he ever married at all, it would be to the dark, sophisticated Sofia, someone he could indulge, feel affection towards but not love, never be in danger of losing his heart. He would never risk falling a victim to the passionate, unquenchable, irresistible kind of love that had over-whelmed his mother, and broken up his family.

'I think——' Emily's voice came out as a dry croak, so she cleared her throat and tried again. 'I think that we should start the walk back to Aphrodite's Baths.'

'Why?' Nikolaos asked, his voice low and his gaze fixing directly on her face.

Emily glanced around nervously. Too late, she realised just how isolated it was up here. And Nikolaos's eyes were taking on that dark glitter that she had already seen a couple of times before. When he had kissed her, wanted to make love to her——

'Because—well, because——' she began very unsteadily, feeling something inside her begin to tremble.

'Because you don't want to be here alone with me?' Nikolaos suggested.

'Of course not,' she lied. 'You don't think that I'm *scared* of you, do you?'

He moved a step closer. 'Perhaps you should be,' he said softly. A self-mocking gleam lit his eyes. 'I'm certainly a little scared of you,' he added, to her absolute amazement.

'Of me?' she echoed, in sheer disbelief. 'You can't be!'

'Why not? When I'm around you, things begin to get a little out of control. And you know how I feel about that.'

'You don't like it,' Emily said, with a small gulp.

'No, I don't,' Nikolaos agreed. He moved still closer. 'The problem is, I *do* like this.'

He was near enough to kiss her now. And he did. A swift, hard kiss that revealed perhaps even more than he had intended.

'You said that you wouldn't do that again,' Emily whispered shakenly. 'We agreed that we'd have a working relationship.'

'I know. And, at the time, I certainly meant it. But you keep making me break all my own rules. And I'm about to break them again,' he added more huskily.

He took another kiss, longer this time, and more intense. Emily took an involuntary step backwards; all her instincts were crying out for her to run away *now*, before he discovered just how much she wanted to give in to this, how long she had secretly been aching for the touch of his lips again.

'I really don't think this is a good idea,' she managed to get out jerkily.

'Of course it isn't. We both know that.' Nikolaos's hand slid into the soft golden mane of her hair, caressed its warmth, then closed around the bright strands, holding her face close to his. 'But, right at this moment, I don't seem to care. And I can't seem to stop,' he added in a much thicker tone of voice.

His mouth covered hers again almost before he had finished speaking. Vague thoughts of resistance drifted through Emily's head, but then drifted right out again, the warmth and pressure of his lips made it impossible to think coherently. Then his fingers untangled themselves from her hair and instead slid over the soft cotton of her dress, tracing the curved shape of her body beneath, touching lightly but hungrily.

Everything inside her seemed to subside into chaos. And such an intensely pleasurable chaos. Emily shivered, despite the heat of the sun and the fire licking through her veins. If she experienced this for too long, she might not be able to live without it —

Nikolaos raised his head and looked directly at her. His dark eyes were brilliant, and his own breathing had become uneven.

'You are dangerous,' he said, the tension clear in his voice. 'I should turn my back on you, walk away, and just keep on walking.'

'Then why aren't you doing it?' Emily somehow found the courage to challenge him.

Their gazes locked and held. Then Nikolaos gave a sudden growl of sheer frustration. 'I've tried. *I have tried.* I've told myself that I didn't want someone with your pale little English face. That uptight little English mind. But I've watched your skin turn gold under our sun, seen you come alive as its heat warmed your heart, and I soon realised that underneath you're just like me, full of hidden fires that would burn and burn if we ever let them get completely out of control.' He swayed even closer, so that she could feel the heat radiating from him, and knew that her own skin was becoming frantically hot. 'You think that I should walk away? So do I. But the trouble is that I want *this* too much,' he finished roughly, and then his mouth was back on hers again, but this time with an intensity that she might have found a little frightening if she hadn't already been responding with an eagerness that amazed her, left her head reeling with the implications of these new revelations.

He kissed her with an ever-growing lack of control, and her own emotions rocketed to new peaks of intensity. This time, his fingers weren't content with moving over her dress, but slid underneath it, and Emily caught her breath sharply as she felt the first touch of his hands against her bare skin. Every nerve in her body silently quivered, and her skin felt almost raw where his fingertips were lightly caressing its silkiness.

With his other free hand, Nikolaos dragged back her golden curls so that his mouth could move restlessly over the nape of her neck. Tendrils of pleasure curled right down to her toes, and her heart thumped even more erratically.

'I can feel you shaking inside,' Nikolaos murmured. 'Deep down, where no one's ever touched you before.'

'I've been touched,' Emily insisted unsteadily, a last vestige of pride wanting to make him believe that she wasn't so naïve that she knew nothing of these things.

'Not in the way that I mean.'

'I'm not some wide-eyed little innocent,' she insisted.

'Yes, you are,' Nikolaos said with absolute certainty. 'You've no idea what this is really all about. No idea what I can do to you,' he went on in a lower, darker voice.

His hand floated upwards, his palm grazed against her breast, and then his fingers curled around her soft flesh, enclosed it, caressed and then gently nipped. A dozen different sensations burst through her, each one more dangerously pleasurable than the last, and Emily's eyes flew open in alarm. Each time he touched her, he was going a little further. And she didn't want to stop him.

To confuse her further, he kissed her again. Not so intensely this time. The touch of his lips was light, gently provocative. His tongue softly probed. He was sharing the touch and taste of himself with her; the dark, exotic, Mediterranean tang of his skin seemed to surround her, the heat of the Cypriot sun seemed to run through his veins. Then his fingers drifted down, beneath the waistband of her dress, across the flat plane of her stomach. Emily closed her eyes and nearly stopped breathing. She knew that she had to make him stop — he was overwhelming her; in a few more seconds she would be ready to give absolutely everything to him, even her soul, and that would be a disaster of cataclysmic proportions because he didn't want her soul — nor her love.

But his fingers were still moving, still exploring, sliding lower and caressing more intimately. Emily swayed faintly; small waves of pleasure were exploding inside her, and *still* he was touching, stroking, caressing —

'No,' she moaned, almost desperately. Then, somehow, she found the strength to say it again. '*No*.'

Nikolaos immediately became still, although he was breathing very unevenly and a dark flush of colour showed beneath the deep tan of his face. 'Why?' he said in a stark tone. 'You want this.'

'I don't want — ' Emily struggled to find the right words, struggled against the rebellious demands of her body, which, for the first time in her adult life, were running almost out of control. 'I don't want — just sex,' she finally got out in a fractured voice. 'Well, yes, I do want it,' she added more honestly, 'but if it's just like this — if there isn't anything else — then it won't mean anything.'

Nikolaos's face darkened. 'And what is the "something else" that you want?' he growled softly. 'Love? You already know that isn't on offer. I've made my feelings on that subject perfectly plain. But I can give you pleasure,' he went on, his black eyes fixing on her with a powerful intensity that made her nerves almost melt. 'In my own way, I can make you happy.'

'But can I make *you* happy?' she said in a low tone.

'I don't think so. Not if the only thing I can ever give you is my body. I've got so much more to give than that — but you don't want it. You don't want any kind of love in your life; you don't trust it. I think that you're even afraid of it because you can't control it.'

They stared at each other for what seemed half a lifetime. Nikolaos was finally the first one to look away.

'You're right, of course,' he said almost angrily. 'I'm not interested in love; I've taught myself to live without it. I *want* to live without it.'

Emily half closed her eyes. She had felt that way once. But not any more. 'People can change,' she said in a soft voice.

'I don't want to change,' Nikolaos said bluntly. 'I want you,' he went on, his black eyes glowing fiercely. 'I've made that very clear. But I can live without you, if I have to. And that's exactly what I'll do, if you won't accept me on my own terms.'

'I can't live with your terms,' Emily said helplessly.

'Then what happened today must never happen again,' Nikolaos said in a grim tone.

She couldn't believe he could cut her out of his life so quickly, so decisively, but before she could shakenly protest he began to speak again.

'Unfortunately, we still have to work together, but in future it would obviously be better if contact between us could be kept to a minimum. In the meantime, I suggest that we return to the hotel immediately. We both have a great deal of work to get on with, and I think it would help the situation if we had something to fully occupy our minds.'

He turned away and strode off, and Emily stumbled after him, unable to believe that it was possible to feel such intense pleasure and such utter misery in such a short space of time.

CHAPTER EIGHT

IT TOOK them an hour and a half to walk back to the Baths of Aphrodite. The wonderful views, the deep, clear blue of the sea, the small inlets ringed by steep cliffs and the birds that wheeled overhead only added to Emily's sadness. A place as beautiful as this was made for lovers, and her love had just been totally rejected. She walked along with her gaze fixed on the hot, dusty ground. She knew that, if she looked up, she would see Nikolaos. And she really didn't think that she could bear to look at him right now.

They finally reached Aphrodite's Baths, and the magic of the picturesque pool with the small streams of water lightly cascading down over the moss-covered limestone briefly enchanted her. Then she realised that Nikolaos had stopped and was looking at her with uncontrolled dark intensity, and she immediately stiffened again.

He spoke for the first time since they had left the Fountain of Love.

'According to legend,' he said in a harsh tone, 'men who had been spurned by Aphrodite went from here to the Spring of Oblivion, where they would take a cold shower that would make them forget her. Perhaps I should do the same.'

Emily's eyes prickled hotly. 'You're making it sound as if everything that happened was *my* fault.'

His black eyes glittened. 'Why not? You knew what was happening between us. You knew as far back as the night of the Limassol carnival, when I first kissed you. Yet you insisted on staying, you still wanted to work for me, you made sure that we spent a lot of time together.'

Emily stared at him in disbelief. 'Are you saying that I *planned* all this? That I *made* it happen?'

'It's not impossible,' Nikolaos said in the same harsh voice. 'Women are so very devious. They know what they want, and they go after it single-mindedly, and to hell with everything — and everyone — else.'

'Women are no more devious than men,' Emily said defensively. 'But you're not really talking about men or women in general, are you, Nikolaos? You're talking about just one woman — your mother!'

His face instantly hardened. 'I don't wish to discuss that particular subject.'

'I think that it's time you did,' she said, somehow finding the courage to ignore the very clear warning signs that radiated from his hostile eyes, the set of his mouth, the tense stance of his body. 'It's your attitude to your mother that's ruining your entire life. Can't you see that?'

'I see that she walked out on her husband and her son,' Nikolaos said fiercely. 'Maybe that's something that's common practice in your country, but here on Cyprus the family comes first, *nothing* is more important.'

'And so her own personal happiness counted for nothing?' Emily challenged him. 'It didn't matter that she was deeply unhappy in her marriage? She was simply expected to endure it for the rest of her life?'

Nikolaos growled angrily. 'You are not Greek, you don't understand.'

'I understand that it must be very hard for any child to forgive his mother for deserting him,' Emily said in a quieter voice. 'But I also know that there has to come a time when all the hatred, the resentment, the animosity has to come to an end. If it doesn't, then it eats you up and destroys you.'

'You're an expert on such matters?' Nikolaos said caustically.

'For a long time, I hated my own father for the violence he inflicted on me, and on my mother,' Emily said, her tone very low. 'But when I grew up I finally realised that such feelings were only self-destructive in the end, that you had to try and understand *why* someone behaved the way they did. And you also had to accept that everyone has faults and makes very bad mistakes.'

Nikolaos was silent for a moment, as if regretting that he had accused her of not knowing what it was like to have had a parent who had destroyed what should have been a happy childhood. Then his darkly tanned features became even more shadowed again, as if old, deeply unhappy memories were suddenly surfacing and surging through him.

'Do you want to know why I can't forgive my mother?' he said abruptly. 'Come with me. I'll show you.'

His hand gripped her wrist and she was forced to follow him as he strode off towards the car park. Nikolaos's own car was waiting for them — Emily realised that he must have arranged for someone to drive it here from the fishing village further along the coast, where they had left it — and he opened the door, then levered her inside.

'Where — where are we going?' she asked rather breathlessly.

'To the Troodos mountains,' he said tersely. 'I'm taking you to visit my father.'

He swung the car off along a narrow road that led

away from the coast, and then steadily began to climb. Emily sat very still and didn't say a word. The car wound its way through the foothills, past small vineyards with rows of vines neatly striping the hillsides, and terraces of fruit bushes. Then the mountains themselves began to close in around them, some almost bare, others covered thickly with trees. Although the temperature didn't fall as the midday sun beat down on them, the air was fresher and scented with the occasional tang of pine. The roads that they followed were sometimes good, sometimes little more than dirt tracks, but Nikolaos seemed to be able to find his way with unerring ease.

The mountains grew higher and a little wilder. Their sides became forested with pines and golden oaks, plane trees, cedars and alders. Black-winged ravens beat their way from branch to branch, and once Emily glimpsed a much larger bird soaring high over the mountainside. She turned to ask Nikolaos what it was, but the grim line of his mouth warned her that he wasn't in the mood for any kind of conversation.

A couple of miles further on, though, the road twisted into a series of spectacular hairpin bends, and they rounded one corner to be confronted by an animal hurriedly crossing the road. Nikolaos swiftly braked, and the animal froze for a few moments and stared at them.

Emily stared back, fascinated by its thick, dark coat with golden highlights where the sun caught it, and its spectacular long, curved horns.

'What is it?' she asked softly.

'A moufflon—a wild sheep,' Nikolaos replied, equally quietly. The animal quickly recovered from its fright, and disappeared into the nearby trees. 'It's found only here, on Cyprus, and it's very rare,' he went on, starting up the car again. 'It's a very long time since I've seen one.'

They drove on, a little more slowly now, as if Nikolaos was already beginning to regret the impulse which had made him set out on this journey. The road wound onwards, past villages which seemed to cling rather precariously to the steep hillsides. The houses were unsophisticated, the streets narrow and often cobbled, and yet they had a warmth and charm uniquely their own. Laden donkeys plodded along the side-streets, taking their time in getting their burdens home. Groups of older women, many of them dressed in black, sat outside their houses in the sun and gossiped, while the men gathered around tables outside small tavernas, drinking coffee, playing backgammon, and putting the world to rights.

Nikolaos finally slowed the car on the outskirts of another, larger village. White-walled houses were clustered around a big church with a couple of high, domed towers. Instead of driving into the centre of the village, though, he turned the car in the other direction, heading towards a house that was set on the very outskirts. As they drew closer, Emily could see that the house had wide, open arches running right along one side, with a balcony overhead and shuttered doors that led into the rooms behind it. A crazy-paving path fringed with sprawling clumps of brilliantly coloured flowers led to the main entrance, with tall, dark, pencil-thin cypresses throwing elegant fingers of shade. The house was set on a flat wedge of land which jutted out from the hillside, and there were dramatically beautiful views of the mountains in all directions.

Nikolaos brought the car to a halt. 'This is my house,' he said briefly.

'It's stunning,' breathed Emily. 'You must love it here.'

'I've never lived here. I come only to visit my father.'

She swallowed hard as she remembered the purpose of this visit. She knew very well that some of the well kept secrets of the Konstantin family were being revealed to her, and she couldn't help wondering why.

She followed him into the house. Inside, the rooms were large and airy, the furniture was dark, solid and comfortable. Emily was staring at the walls, though. They were painted in pale, tranquil colours, but very little of them could be seen because they were covered in paintings.

Each painting was exquisitely detailed, and glowed with warmth and colour. Many were landscapes, mainly of the mountains, some were portraits, and a few were of the house itself, and the village. The artist obviously found his inspiration on his own doorstep.

Emily wanted just to stand and look at them, but Nikolaos's hand was already gripping her elbow, forcing her forward again. He led her through into the next room, where an older, dark-haired woman came forward to meet them.

'Nikolaos!' she said with a smile. 'I thought that I heard your car.'

Emily knew at once that this had to be another member of the Konstantin family. She had the familiar dark, handsome looks and confident presence.

'Aunt Evi,' Nikolaos greeted her crisply. 'I've come to see my father. How is he?'

'Very well,' said his aunt. 'And you must be Emily,' she went on. 'I've been wanting to meet you.'

'How do you know who I am?' asked Emily, in surprise.

'She's met up with Aunt Anna,' Nikolaos answered

for her, with a touch of resignation. 'You'll soon find
out that it's impossible to keep any secrets in this
family.'

Emily could feel her face getting hotter as she
wondered exactly what these two aunts of Nikolaos's
had said to each other. Nikolaos was already speaking
again, though, drawing his aunt's attention away from
her. 'Is my father in his usual place?'

'Of course,' said Aunt Evi. 'He'll be pleased to see
you.'

'Will he?' said Nikolaos, his tone suddenly edged
with a thread of bitterness. 'And how will I know?'

'Oh, Nikolaos,' said his aunt with sudden compassion, and she reached out her hand to him, but
Nikolaos had already moved away, as if he couldn'
bear to be the object of anyone's pity.

'Come,' he said to Emily, a trifle roughly. Then he
walked out of the room, and Emily hurried after him.

He led her to a large terrace at the back of the house
which had magnificent views of the surrounding mountains, and the village.

An easel was set up at the end of the terrace, and in
front of it, painting intently, stood a tall man with
broad shoulders and grey-flecked hair.

'Hello, Father,' said Nikolaos in a low voice, as if he
didn't want to startle him.

Yannis Konstantin turned round, gave them an
uncertain smile, and then went straight back to his
painting. He had a strong face, but it bore very little
resemblance to his son's. It was Eléni, his mother
whom Nikolaos took after, Eléni with the black
expressive eyes, dark, glossy hair and sensual mouth.

'This is Emily,' Nikolaos went on in the same level
tone. 'I believe Aunt Evi told you about her. I wanted
you to meet her.'

This time, Yannis Konstantin didn't even acknowledge that he had heard them. Instead, he went on painting, steadily and intently. Nikolaos touched Emily's arm, and signalled that they should go back into the house.

Once they were inside and out of earshot, she turned to him in bewilderment. 'Doesn't he *recognise* you?'

'I don't know,' Nikolaos said, his face suddenly very drawn. 'He's been like this since my mother left. He never speaks, doesn't respond to anyone, not even Aunt Evi who looks after him. He simply eats, sleeps and paints. Aunt Evi says that he's happy and contented. I hope that she's right, but there's no way I can know for certain.'

Emily's heart contracted as she saw the deep pain in his eyes. 'His paintings are very beautiful,' she said softly. 'Only someone with a soul that's at peace could produce work like that.'

'He's also a very successful painter,' Nikolaos said, a sudden note of pride in his voice. 'I've arranged several exhbitions of his work, and people are beginning to collect his pictures. Of course, he doesn't know about that—nothing that happens outside this house seems to concern him any more,' he went on, the brittle edge back in his tone again. 'But if he ever comes back to us again, decides to live in the real world, at least he'll know that he's achieved something.'

'I like that,' Emily said, nodding gently. 'I like it that you care enough to make him a successful man, and let other people see how brilliant he is.'

'Of course I care,' Nikolaos said roughly. 'He's my father.' Then he turned away rather abruptly, but not before Emily had seen the sudden brightness in his eyes.

They stayed at the house for another hour after that.

Nikolaos spent some more time with his father, while Emily talked with Aunt Evi, learning more about the lonely and yet apparently not unhappy years that Yannis Konstantin had spent at this house, producing his exquisite paintings. He had lost his wife and turned his face away from the world, but seemed to have found some consolation in his own brilliant talent.

When she and Nikolaos finally left, they drove back down the winding mountain roads in silence. They reached the coast just as the sun was dipping down towards the horizon and the sky, the sea, the land was bathed in a golden light that gradually warmed to dazzling shades of red and orange before fading into a softer, more tranquil glow as night quickly approached.

Emily realised that the road Nikolaos had taken had brought them out at Coral Bay. In the gathering twilight, she could see the distinctive shape of his villa, the pale walls catching and reflecting the last faint rays of colour from the sinking sun. Then he turned into the entrance and brought the car to a halt.

'Come inside,' he said, rather roughly.

Emily thought that he must want to speak to Aunt Anna before continuing on to Paphos. Perhaps there was some message he needed to pass on from his other aunt, Evi.

Inside the villa, though, it seemed silent and empty. No lights were on, and Nikolaos switched on just one small lamp in the main room, which left the corners still full of dark shadows.

'Has—has your aunt already gone to bed?' Emily asked, suddenly feeling rather nervous.

Nikolaos looked at her. 'Aunt Anna isn't here,' he said in a soft tone. 'She's gone to Limassol for a few days. Her excuse was that she needed to do some shopping, but I think that she's actually gone because she wants to make some enquiries about you. She wants to meet the people at the hotel whom you worked with and made friends with.'

'Why?' Emily said in surprise.

'Aunt Anna is incurably curious. She likes to know everything about everyone. And since meeting you — and no doubt jumping to the wrong conclusion — she wants to know more about you. How better than asking people who know you?'

She chewed her lip warily. 'What do you mean, she's jumped to the wrong conclusion? And *what* does she want to find out about me?'

'Whether you would make a suitable wife. For me,' he added in an oddly self-mocking voice.

'For you?' Emily's eyes shot wide open with shock. Then she recovered slightly. 'But you don't want a wife,' she reminded him slightly bitterly. 'At least, not one who will make you feel, make you want, make you come *alive*. You want a relationship where you're always in control, where you're never going to have to give anything of yourself. You want a wife you won't love, so that you won't ever be in danger of being hurt.'

'Yes, that's what I want,' Nikolaos said tightly. 'And I can't have that with you, can I, Emily? You came here as a pale-faced, uptight little English girl, but the island of love has changed you; look at you — ' his dark gaze slid over her with sudden hunger ' — you're tanned, healthy, full of life, full of love. And you're longing to give that love to someone. But I don't want it, Emily. *I don't want it.*'

But he looked as if he desperately wanted something from her, as the hunger in his eyes deepened and he took a couple of steps towards her.

Emily immediately began to back away. 'No, don't do this,' she almost pleaded. 'You're right, I want so

much, too much, I know that, but if I can't have
everything then it would be better to have nothing at
all. Please, Nikolaos, just let me go——'

His eyes flared with a new light. 'Do you know what
it does to me when you say my name? Probably not, or
you'd say it more often.'

'Nikolaos——' she said, without thinking, then bit
her lip hard as she saw him come a little nearer to
losing his self-control.

Outside, the velvet darkness of the night had fallen
over the bay, and only the faintest light shimmered on
the sea as the thin sliver of a new moon slid into the
sky. Inside the room, dusky shadows surrounded them
as they stood just outside the pale pool of light thrown
out by the small lamp. It was enough for Emily to see
Nikolaos's face, though; see all the conflicting emotions
chasing across his taut features.

He shook his head very slowly, almost despairingly.
'I've never been in this situation before,' he muttered.
'I've always been able to walk away from a relationship,
cut myself off from it before I got too involved.'

'You can still walk away,' Emily said in a low, shaky
voice. 'It isn't too late.'

'Oh, but it is,' Nikolaos said softly. 'Tonight, I can't
walk away from anything.'

He moved towards her again, and Emily knew that if
she let him touch her, then she would be hurtling
headlong into the kind of trouble that could wreck her
life completely. She also knew why Nikolaos was in this
oddly uncontrolled and vulnerable mood. The visit to
his father had left his nerves and emotions raw and
twisted; he desperately needed solace of some kind,
and tonight he could only get it here, with her.

And yes, he certainly wanted that solace, wanted
her; those dark, passionate eyes burned in the dim light

in the same way that his fingers would burn against her skin, if she let him touch her.

He was so close now, she could feel his breath against her face, warm and fresh, she could smell the tang of his skin. Emily felt helpless against the force of his need. And an answering ache was stirring inside of her, echoes of the desire he had woken in her earlier, when he had kissed her at the Fountain of Love.

The Fountain of Love, she repeated to herself slightly dizzily. What a fool she had been to go there with this man! She had already been under his spell, and now she felt as if she had been touched by the finger of Aphrodite herself; all the pent-up love that had been bottled up inside of her for so long was springing free, and she couldn't do anything to stop it; Nikolaos wasn't the only one who was beginning to spin wildly out of control—

His mouth hovered only inches away; she felt him make one last effort to draw back, and fail. Then the pressure of his lips made her breath catch in her throat, and the dark intensity of the kiss seemed to leave her body boneless.

Nikolaos briefly released her and lifted her head. 'You said that my father's paintings showed that his soul was at peace. Well, that's what I need—a soul that's at peace, even if it's only for one night.' He gave a twisted smile. 'Does that sound selfish and self-centred? I suppose that it does. But I don't care. For just one night of my life, I want to be free.'

'And do you care what I want?' Emily said in a low tone.

He shook her a little roughly. 'You know that I do. But you want exactly the same thing that I do.'

'No,' she insisted. She wanted love and he wouldn't—couldn't—give her that.

'Yes,' Nikolaos said inexorably. His palm slid over her hot skin, his mouth brushed against her bruised lips again. 'Whatever we both want for the future, tonight we both simply want this.' His fingers dipped suddenly, beneath the thin material of her dress to the small, hard peaks of her breasts. 'You can lie to me,' he murmured, 'but your body can't.' She shuddered violently as he touched her, and the shadow of a smile touched the taut corners of his mouth. 'You want more of this. And from no one else, just me.'

'You're so arrogant,' Emily accused helplessly, knowing that it was useless to deny that small, flickering tongues of fire were already running along all of her nerve-ends.

'Only where you're concerned,' Nikolaos told her roughly. 'And you've every right to feel just as arrogant. No one else has ever been able to make me behave like this.'

His fingers found the small buttons that fastened the front of her dress, they quickly, expertly undid them, and then his palm rested against the warm silkiness of her skin.

Emily made a small sound in her throat, but it wasn't a protest. She had already gone way past the point where she could fight this. She adored this man too much, and right now it didn't matter that he didn't *want* her adoration, it was enough that he wanted something from her.

Nikolaos's hands began to move again, very gently this time — she hadn't thought that he could ever be this gentle. They left a melting pleasure in their wake, slow, slow waves of an exquisite sensation that gradually intensified as his fingers explored more intimately.

His mouth covered hers again, as if he wanted — needed — to taste her, and his hands busied themselves with the last of the fastenings of her dress, so that it slid softly from her shoulders. Then he bent his head to the soft swell of her breast and everything swiftly began to slide into confusion — his own breathing quickened and became unsteady, his hands weren't so gentle now, but increasingly demanding.

'One night when we can both have what we want,' he muttered, the words muffled because his mouth was still buried against her hot, damp skin.

He picked her up and swiftly carried her into the bedroom. There were no lights switched on, and in the darkness Emily heard his own clothes being quickly discarded. Then she found herself lying on the bed beside him, the musky scent of his skin dizzying her senses, his hot skin already brushing restlessly, urgently against hers, his hands, his mouth moved over her, his touch scalded her, his lips hungrily explored the softness of her breasts and roughly teased the hard, rawly sensitive tips, then trailed down over the quivering muscles of her stomach so that his tongue could lick the silky inner skin of her thighs, until Emily felt as if her entire world was about to explode and fall apart around her.

Then Nikolaos raised his head and his voice sounded almost fierce in the darkness. 'Touch *me*,' he ordered thickly, and he gripped her hand and pulled it towards him.

Immediately, Emily obeyed. She was discovering just how frighteningly pleasurable it could be to obey a man's commands.

His body was well shaped, hard and hot. His muscles stood out tautly under his smooth, damp skin as the caresses of her hands, tentative at first and then more confident, caused a new tension to quiver through him. She loved the feel of him, the sensual friction of skin against skin, the pleasure that it gave her to give *him* pleasure.

'Enough!' Nikolaos muttered at last, his voice little more than a fractured gasp. But Emily didn't want to stop; she was fascinated — and awed — by the response of this powerful, controlled man to the soft touch of her fingers. She stroked him lightly, almost mischievously, forcing him to catch hold of her wrists and hold her hands away from him for a few frantic seconds while he fought to hold on to the last few strands of his self-control.

It was a battle that was already lost, though. They both knew it, and Emily's arms were already slipping around him, drawing him closer. She felt his shuddering response, and then his heavy weight as he turned towards her, pulled her up tight against him, let his hands run over her in one last powerful, possessive caress, and then swiftly, easily, eased her into the ultimate intimacy.

A faint tremor of shock ran through Emily, and a sudden, unexpected shyness. She had wanted — ached — for this, and yet part of her still hadn't been quite ready for it. She hid her face against his shoulder. Nikolaos's voice murmured soothingly even as his body began to move again, driven on by desire that he had no power to stop.

The familiar sound of his voice reassured her, relaxed her, and with the relaxation came the realisation that her own body was already responding again with its own swift waves of pleasure, her skin was growing as hot as his, her nerve-ends as raw. The intensity of feeling swiftly grew; it began to make her feel dizzy. She held on to Nikolaos very tightly; she needed to hold on to something real in a world that was beginning to dissolve into a great spinning whirlpool of hot, liquid pleasure.

And through all the turmoil, the heat, sweat and his own fierce desire, Nikolaos seemed to know exactly when the turbulent sensations he was creating spiralled to a tense, almost unbearable height; knew the exact moment when the final thrust of his shuddering body caused that pleasure to break and cascade over her in a bewildering flood of intense delight.

Emily heard him say her name, again and again, as the last spasms of pleasure vibrated through him. No one had ever said her name quite like that before; she closed her eyes and let it add to the overwhelming sweetness of the moment.

The pleasure slowly faded until only faint echoes of it remained, but the sweetness lingered on. Nikolaos didn't move for a long while, but then he finally eased himself up on one elbow and looked down at her in the darkness. His hand moved restlessly over her for a while, only finally becoming still again as it curled round the softness of her breast.

'I wanted a soul that would be at peace,' he said in an uneven voice. 'But now I feel as if I'll never be at peace again in my entire life.'

'Love isn't peaceful,' Emily said softly.

'Which is why I don't want it in my life. But I have to have it tonight,' Nikolaos said almost hoarsely. 'I *have* to.'

His hand began to move again, and his body pressed against hers with new urgency, already aroused by her closeness. Emily silently welcomed him back into her arms because, for this one night at least, he belonged to her. In return, she would give him anything he wanted. And something that he didn't want — her love.

* * *

They finally slept for a couple of hours just before dawn, a deep dreamless sleep that swallowed them up.

When Emily finally woke up again, for a few moments she couldn't remember why her body should feel so heavy and languid. Then she suddenly remembered *everything*, and sat bolt upright.

The bedroom was empty; there was no sign of Nikolaos. There were two dents in the pillow, though, where two heads had lain close together. Very close together. Emily gave a small shiver as she remembered just how close they had been.

Where was he now, though? Very slowly, she got out of bed and walked over to the door. Had he simply gone? Left her here on her own? She shivered again as she considered that awful possibility.

Then she heard the sound of voices. A man's and a woman's. The man's was clearly recognisable as Nikolaos. And the woman's? It sounded familiar, but Emily couldn't seem to think straight this morning, couldn't make her memory produce a face to fit the voice.

A bathrobe was draped over the end of the bed, obviously left there for her by Nikolaos. Emily pulled it on, ran her fingers through her tangled curls, and then opened the door.

Her head still felt dazed, her limbs heavy with the pleasure that had racked every inch of her last night. Without really thinking what she was doing, she headed towards the sound of the voices.

She pushed open the door to the large, sun-filled room with its glorious views of the bay. Inside, she found Nikolaos standing by the window, already fully dressed. And standing opposite him was Sofia.

Emily felt a distinct wave of shock as she saw the other woman. What was she doing here? Then she became starkly aware of the contrast between herself and the Cypriot girl. As always, Sofia was dressed in a simple but very sophisticated style. This morning, she wore pale linen trousers and a silk blouse, her nails were immaculately varnished, and expertly applied make-up emphasised her handsome features and dark, beautiful eyes.

Emily stood there, barefoot, her hair tumbling haphazardly to her shoulders, and felt Sofia's hostile gaze fixed on her. The colour rose in Emily's face because she knew that it must be very obvious to the other woman what had happened here last night.

It was impossible to tell from Nikolaos's own face what he was thinking. His eyes were cool and withdrawn as he faced his cousin.

'It's very early in the morning, Sofia,' he said in a flat voice. 'And you haven't told me yet what you are doing here.'

'I have some news for you,' Sofia said, her eyes bright with suppressed emotion. 'If Emily hasn't already told you?' she added.

'Told me what?' Nikolaos demanded with sudden impatience.

'That your mother is here, on Cyprus. She's staying at a house just outside Paphos.'

Nikolaos became very silent and still, and Emily's own heart almost stopped beating.

'How do you know this?' he said at last, in a very carefully controlled voice.

'I met her last night. It was quite by chance; I came to Paphos to spend the evening with some friends, and saw Eléni walking along the street. We spoke for quite some time,' Sofia went on. 'In fact, we had a very interesting conversation.'

'And why should Emily have been able to tell me

that my mother is here?' Nikolaos said in a tone that Emily suddenly found quite terrifying.

Triumph flashed at last in Sofia's eyes. 'Because she has known for a couple of days that Eléni is staying near Paphos. She has met her and spoken to her. In fact, she even agreed to help Eléni meet you. Your mother and Emily seem to be quite good friends, Nikolaos.'

Nikolaos slowly turned to Emily, and the look on his face made her heart turn to stone. He was never going to forgive her for this deception, especially since he had broken all his own rules about personal privacy and confided to her his own very private bitterness towards his mother. Everything that had happened between them last night had just been destroyed by Sofia's deliberately malicious words.

Emily felt her world beginning to fall apart around her, and knew that she would never be able to put it back together again.

CHAPTER NINE

Nikolaos's gaze fixed on Emily with a coldness that she found far more distressing than a fierce outburst of anger.

'You have met my mother?' he said in a dangerously soft voice.

'It was quite by accident,' Emily said almost in a whisper. 'And I was going to tell you.'

'When?' he demanded more harshly.

'I—I was waiting for the right time.'

Sofia gave a brief, edged laugh which broke into their conversation. 'It seems to me that you've had plenty of time to talk during the past day—and night.'

Nikolaos spun round, as if only just remembering that she was there. 'I think that it's time for you to leave, Sofia,' he said tersely.

Sofia's face instantly changed. 'Leave?' she said, her voice fracturing slightly on that one word.

'You've said what you came here to say,' Nikolaos said icily, looking at her now as if she were a stranger. 'Accomplished what you intended to accomplish.'

'But I didn't mean—I didn't want——' Sofia stammered, her face first turning very pale, and then colouring as brightly as a young schoolgirl's, all her poise and sophistication suddenly deserting her.

'To turn me against you?' Nikolaos finished for her with ruthless accuracy. 'But you haven't. You've simply reminded me of something that I very nearly forgot for a while. No woman can be trusted. You all play games with other people's lives, you go after what *you* want, and to hell with everything — and everyone — else.'

'We are not all like that,' Emily protested at once.

His dark eyes fixed on her with a fierceness that immediately reduced her to nerve-racked silence. Then he turned back to his cousin.

'Leave my house, Sofia,' he ordered. 'And I would rather that we didn't meet again for quite some time.'

It was the worst punishment that he could have inflicted on her. Sofia flinched as if he had physically hit her. Then she slowly turned round and left the room, her shoulders slumped in acceptance of the awful fact that she had lost Nikolaos forever.

Emily waited tensely for him to order her to leave as well. She could hardly bear to hear him say the words, but the last few dregs of her pride and courage helped her to stand straight and steady.

Nikolaos didn't say a single word, though. Instead, he wheeled round and strode from the room without even looking at her.

When he had gone, she sank down on to the nearest chair, her legs trembling. For a few moments, she wished that she had never spoken to Eléni; certainly wished that she had never agreed to help her. Then Emily remembered the stark misery in the eyes of Nikolaos's mother, and knew that she couldn't have just turned away from her. If Nikolaos could only be persuaded to meet his mother, if he would just look into those dark, stricken eyes and see what her decision to walk out on her family had cost her, then surely he would relent?

Emily gave a small sigh. But perhaps not — Nikolaos had so much pride. And a pain that he refused to admit; pain that had stretched all through the years of his adult life, right back into the highly impressionable years of early adolescence.

And now he would never trust her again. He thought that she and his mother had been conspiring together behind his back, and that was something he could never forgive, particularly after that visit to his father, when he had let her see how his mother's desertion had affected his family.

Very, very slowly, walking as if she were an old woman, Emily went back into the bedroom and dressed. She didn't shower. She could still smell the musky scent of Nikolaos on her skin and she didn't want to wash it away, not yet. It was a poignant reminder of the intimacy they had shared for such a short time, and would almost certainly never share again.

She knew that she should leave the villa, return to Paphos. Instead, though, she found herself following the steep path that led down to the beach. Although she felt as if she had been up for hours it was still, incredibly, early morning, and very few people had ventured down on to the wide sweep of beach that filled the inner curve of the great bay. The pink-tinged sand was already warm beneath her bare feet, however, and the sea sparkled with a crystal-clearness under the bright rays of the sun.

Then Emily saw the tall, dark figure standing motionless some distance away, staring out to sea.

She swallowed very hard; then she began to walk steadily forward. Walked towards the dark figure.

Nikolaos didn't turn and look at her, not even when she was finally standing only a few feet away. She knew that he was very aware of her presence, though. The absolute stillness of his body betrayed him.

She realised that she was standing in exactly the same

way, hardly daring even to breathe. It took an enormous effort to take the last couple of steps that brought her to stand in front of him.

His face was closed, his dark eyes shuttered so that they revealed absolutely no emotion. It was hard to believe that this was the same man who had made love to her with such passionate intensity last night.

'What do you want me to say?' Emily said at last, in a low voice. 'That I'm sorry?'

'I hardly think that an apology would cover the situation,' Nikolaos replied flatly, after a long silence which had made her think that he wasn't going to answer her at all.

'Oh, you're so stubborn!' she suddenly burst out. 'Why can't you give way just a little, be willing to meet people at least halfway?'

'By "people", I assume that you're referring to my mother?' he said coldly.

'Of course I am. Look, I know that I should have told you that I'd met her, but can't you at least understand why I didn't?'

'No,' came his deliberately detached reply.

'Because I knew that you'd react like this! And the awful thing is that you're hurting yourself as much as you're hurting her, because I think that you *want* to meet her. You certainly need to! You're never going to be a complete human being, Nikolaos, until you've faced up to this, confronted all the old painful ghosts of your childhood.'

His black eyes began to glitter as his façade of self-control started to slip.

'How dare you tell me what I need to do? You know nothing about it. Nothing!'

'Of course I do,' Emily retorted with equal vehemence. 'Parts of my own childhood were a nightmare —

ysical abuse is one of the most frightening things that
happen to you when you're young. But if my father
re alive today I wouldn't turn my back on him. I'd
nt to talk to him, make him understand the harm he
to me, the damage he caused. And I'd want *him* to
k to *me*, so that I'd at least know why he did it, what
ssures forced him into it. It's only by talking and
derstanding — and forgiving — that we can finally put
ll behind us, and get on with our lives.'

I am getting on with my life,' Nikolaos said tautly.
e managed very well during the twenty years since
mother left, and I see no reason why I shouldn't
tinue to do so in the future.'

But you can't love anyone,' Emily cried.

I love my family,' he countered at once.

I know. You'd do anything for them, help them in
and every way you could, if they needed it. But
t isn't what I'm talking about.'

Of course it isn't,' Nikolaos said, his dark gaze
denly fixing on her own flushed face. 'You mean
t I can't love *you*.' The sensual line of his mouth
dened. 'All women want love. Why can't any of you
ieve that you can live without it?'

Because if you don't have some kind of love in your
, then you're only existing. I've understood that
ce I came here, to Cyprus. The island of love — '
gave a small, strained smile ' — the home of
hrodite — how can you live here, and not believe in
e?'

He didn't answer her. His eyes were no longer blank;
could see the conflict that raged behind their dark
ade. As if suddenly aware that she could see his
er turmoil, Nikolaos abruptly turned away from her.

I don't want to meet my mother, and I'd prefer to
as little of you as possible in the future,' he said in

a tight voice. 'Regarding the terms of Dimitri's w
some legal solution will have to be found and ot
arrangements made.'

'Oh, you stupid man,' she said bitterly. 'You're go
to throw it all away, aren't you?'

'I've simply made a decision that needed to be ma
I believe that is my prerogative.'

'It's certainly your prerogative to lead a lon
unhappy life, if that's what you want,' said Emily, w
more courage than she knew she possessed. Then, w
her shoulders held unnaturally high and her eyes bli
ing away a threatening flurry of tears, she turned
steadily walked away from him. She looked back o
once — she couldn't stop herself — and saw that he
rigidly staring out to sea again, a dark, passionate n
who lived on the sunlit island of love, but refused to
himself feel love.

Back at Paphos, she discovered that the H
Konstantin had lost all of its charms. Oh, she
worked hard — harder than ever; it was better t
having any free time to think, to *feel*. But all the
had gone out of it, and she worked mechanically; it
just a way of filling in all the long, empty hours.

Her contact with Nikolaos was virtually non-exist
For the moment, at least, he remained at the hote
ensuring that the hotel didn't collapse under her in
perienced management, she thought bitterly — but
communications from him came through his secreta

Emily had thought that she had explored all the bl
depths of misery after her mother's and Dimi
deaths, but this was an entirely new kind of heartbre
And, as far as she could see, it was going to go on
on. That was a quite appalling prospect, and one
threatened to overwhelm her at times.

What could she do about it, though? Go back home
England? But, although it was something that she
d never expected to happen when she had first come
re, England no longer felt like home. After just a
w short months, home was here, on this island
enched in sun and ancient myths and legends. She
ved its blue seas, hot beaches and green forests, its
illiantly spectacular sunsets, the perfume of its spring
wers, the sweet ripeness of its fruit and, of course,
e friendliness of its people.

By the end of the week, though, she knew that she
uldn't stay unless something changed. And nothing
uld change of its own accord; she had to *make* it
ppen. An idea was already beginning to form inside
r head, but just the thought of what she was contem-
ating was so unnerving that she kept shying away
m it. There was probably only one chance in a
ndred that it would work out; it was far more likely
it she would destroy everything forever. And it
uld need very careful planning, there were so many
ngs that could go wrong.

Emily shivered a little, despite the heat. If she went
ead with her crazy idea, it would need every last bit
her courage to see it through. On the other hand,
e didn't think that any of them could go on for very
ich longer with the way things were. No one was
ppy, all of them locked away in their own separate,
happy lives. At least this would give her a small
ance to put some things right.

She picked up the phone and dialled the number that
ni had given her. She was relieved when Eléni
rself answered.

It's Emily Peterson,' Emily said nervously. 'Do you
member me?'

Of course I do,' Eléni said with sudden eagerness.

'Have you managed to speak to Nikolaos? Has
agreed to see me?'

'I think that I can arrange for you to meet him
Emily said, choosing her words carefully.

'When?' said Eléni at once. 'Can it be soon? I c
only stay on Cyprus for a couple of more days.'

'This afternoon,' Emily told her, after taking a ve
deep breath. 'I'll arrange it for this afternoon, if tha
all right with you.'

'Yes, it's fine,' said Eléni, and Emily could hear t
small tremor of emotion in her voice. 'What tir
should I come?'

'If you can get here at exactly three o'clock, I'll
waiting for you at the main entrance.'

'I'll be there,' promised Eléni. 'And—thank yo
You know what this means to me.'

Emily immediately felt guilty because Elé
obviously thought that Nikolaos had agreed to t
meeting. She bit her lip and was about to blurt out t
truth, but Eléni had already put the receiver dow
Emily reached out to redial the number, but th
stopped. She knew that she was gambling with oth
people's lives, but sometimes the only thing to do w
to take a reckless chance.

She spent a couple of minutes trying to control h
breathing and slow her racing pulse. Then she ra
Nikolaos's office, knowing that she would get throu
to him directly since his secretary was off sick today.

The familiar, authoritative sound of his voice as
answered the phone made her skin break out in
sudden flush of heat.

'I—I want to make an appointment to see you t
afternoon, at three o'clock,' she finally managed to ş
out.

There was a long silence before he at last answer

her. 'I can spare you a few minutes if you wish to discuss something important. I'm having lunch with a business colleague, followed by a short meeting, but I can be back here by three.' His voice sounded more strained than she could ever remember hearing it.

'Thank you,' she said, swallowing hard. She listened for a few more moments to the sound of his breathing, more audible and much faster than usual. Then she put down the phone, her own lungs feeling very constricted.

Later on that morning, she watched Nikolaos leave the hotel for his luncheon appointment. Then she slipped up to his office. She went at once to the small cupboard where he kept his keys. It was locked, of course, but she used her own master key to open it. It took her just a few seconds to slip all the keys off their hooks, and put them into her pocket. Then she relocked the cupboard and, her heart still thundering, hurried out of the office.

All she had to do now was to wait for three o'clock. The hours went past so slowly that she sometimes thought that the hands of her watch were actually standing still. At last, though, it was time for her to go down and meet Eléni.

When she reached the hotel foyer, she thought for a few nerve-racking moments that Eléni hadn't come. Then she saw her standing beside a large potted palm, half hidden by the large, graceful fronds.

Eléni stepped forward when she saw Emily. 'I'm so very nervous,' she admitted. 'I was almost too terrified to come.'

Emily was quite certain that Eléni couldn't be half as terrified as *she* was. She tried to hide all her surging fears, though, and gave Eléni what she hoped was an encouraging smile.

'Come on, I'll take you up to Nikolaos's office.'

'How does he feel about meeting me?' Eléni asked anxiously as they got into the lift.

'I — don't know,' Emily replied evasively. At the same time, she was being racked by doubts. Did she have any right to be doing this? But it was too late now to turn back. How could she possibly tell Eléni the whole thing had been her idea from the very start? That Nikolaos had known — still knew — absolutely nothing about it?

They reached the floor of Nikolaos's office, and Emily's mouth became completely dry. Then they were finally standing outside his door, and Emily turned to Eléni.

'Just go straight in,' she said steadily.

She saw Eléni's fingers tremble as she reached for the handle. Then she turned it, pushed the door open and walked inside.

Nikolaos was sitting behind his desk, going through some papers, and Emily caught just a brief glimpse of his face as he looked up and saw his mother. It was a sudden rage of conflicting emotions, which swiftly coalesced into a dark anger as he saw Emily standing outside.

'Why have you done this?' he demanded fiercely, getting swiftly to his feet.

Emily didn't answer. Instead, she quickly closed the door and, using her master key, locked it, trapping Nikolaos inside with Eléni.

An instant later, she heard him hammer against it. 'Emily, open this door *at once*,' he roared at her, his voice white hot with fury.

Her legs were shaking — in fact, her whole body was quivering, every nerve was absolutely raw — but she didn't falter.

'No,' she said resolutely. 'It's going to stay locked for one hour. And you won't be able to open it, either; I've taken all your master keys.'

'What the hell do you think you're doing?' he demanded fiercely.

'I'm forcing you to make a choice. You and your mother can either sit in silence for the next hour, or you can begin talking to one another.'

'You've no right to force us into this situation,' Nikolaos said furiously.

'No, I haven't,' she agreed, her own voice almost cracking up with nerves. 'But I've done it, and I intend to go through with it. You've got one hour,' she reminded him.

'When I get out of here —' Nikolaos began threateningly, but Emily was already walking away, because she was afraid that if she stayed any longer then she might weaken, and let them out.

She could hardly believe that she had actually done it, locked them in there together. She had had absolutely no right to do something like that; only the unshakeable conviction that Nikolaos and Eléni needed to find some kind of peace together, so that they could get on with their lives.

And what if it all went horribly wrong? If they came out of that room hating each other — and hating *her* for having caused an even deeper rift in their relationship?

Emily bit her lip hard and glanced at her watch. Only five minutes had passed since she had walked away from that door. How on earth was she going to get through the rest of the hour?

She paced restlessly around her own office, asked one of the staff to bring her up a cup of coffee, but then couldn't drink it. Half an hour dragged past, another endless fifteen minutes crawled by, and then, finally, the hour was up.

Emily crept back to Nikolaos's office, her ears straining for any sounds that would give her a clue to what was going on inside that locked room. She could hear nothing, though. Either Nikolaos and Eléni were sitting in total silence, or they were talking so softly that their voices couldn't be heard through the thickness of the door.

Her fingers fumbling nervously, Emily slid the key into the lock. She turned it and heard the lock click back; then she turned round and ran, too scared to face Nikolaos when he opened that door.

She fled back to the safety of her own office. Except that it wasn't safe, of course. There wasn't anywhere in this hotel — in fact, probably on the entire island — where she could hide away from him.

Emily paced restlessly over to the window and stood there for a long while with her hot forehead pressed against the glass. Then her blue eyes suddenly opened very wide as she saw Eléni walk out from the front entrance of the hotel. A couple of seconds later, they became as big as saucers as she saw Nikolaos follow her out.

Holding her breath, she watched the two of them stand there for a few more minutes, quietly talking. Nikolaos's face looked calm, and there was a hint of a grave smile on Eléni's beautiful mouth. Emily felt her whole body sag with relief. They weren't screaming at each other, or standing in icy silence. It looked as if her gamble might just have paid off.

Eléni finally got into a waiting taxi, and Nikolaos turned and walked back into the hotel. Emily instantly grew very tense again. Whatever had happened in that locked room between Nikolaos and his mother, one thing was very certain. Nikolaos was going to have plenty to say on the subject of Emily's own part in the affair.

She didn't have to wait for very long. Just a couple of minutes later, the door to her office was thrown open and Nikolaos strode in.

'I ought to wring your interfering little neck,' he growled at her.

'I know,' she mumbled apologetically. 'I had absolutely no right to do what I did.'

'No, you certainly didn't!' Yet his dark eyes weren't as fierce as she had expected. 'Especially since you know very well how I feel about people interfering in my personal life.'

'You don't like it,' Emily said in a small voice.

'And yet you still do it.'

'I can't seem to help it. When I see that something's wrong, I just have to try and put it right.'

'Even when you've been specifically told not to meddle?'

Emily gave a small sigh. 'Yes, I'm afraid so.' Then she looked at him anxiously. 'You did speak to your mother? I mean, speak to her properly? You didn't shout at her, or upset her?'

'Of course not,' Nikolaos said at once. 'What kind of man do you think I am?'

'A very stubborn one,' she said. Then she bit her lip. That hadn't been a very wise thing to say.

'And also very lenient,' he pointed out. 'A lot of men would want to punish you very severely for what you did.'

'You're — you're not going to punish me?' Emily said with new hopefulness.

He gave another small growl. 'It doesn't look like it.'

'And everything's all right? I mean, between you and Eléni?'

'Of course it isn't all right,' Nikolaos said, making her heart sink right down again. 'Too much has happened, too much damage has been done. What did you think, that you could wave a magic wand and put everything right overnight?' Then, seeing her totally downcast face, he went on more quietly, 'But we have agreed to meet again before she leaves Cyprus. And I think that we will keep in touch, in the future. More than that I can't promise you at the moment.'

Emily's face instantly brightened again. 'It's enough.' Then her brows drew lightly together. 'But—what about your father? Will Eléni also go and see him?'

'We discussed it,' Nikolaos said, after a short pause. 'But my father lives very much in a world of his own. You've seen him, you understand how he is. We decided that, for now at least, it might be better to leave that world undisturbed.'

'Yes, I think you're probably right,' she said slowly.

Nikolaos gave a faint, dry smile. 'At last I seem to have done something that you approve of.'

'Oh, no, I approve of everything you've done today,' she said earnestly. 'I didn't think—well, I didn't know how it was going to turn out. I thought you might have too much pride—that you might refuse even to *talk* to Eléni—or that you would half kill me afterwards, for what I'd done.'

'Ah, yes,' he said thoughtfully, 'I seem to remember that I had a strong inclination at one time to wring your neck.' He moved closer and his fingers slid round the slim column of her throat. Emily gulped audibly. Then his fingers lightly caressed the soft, vulnerable skin, finally resting against her wildly beating pulse.

'Why do I let you interfere in my life?' he murmured.

'Meddle in my personal affairs? Turn my entire existence upside-down? Keep me awake at night?'

'K-keep you awake?' Emily stuttered.

Nikolaos's fingers tightened their grip, drew her face nearer to his own. 'But you know that you do,' he told her, his eyes beginning to glitter very brightly. 'I think that you know *exactly* what you do to me.'

'I—I've hardly even seen you for the past week,' she protested.

'We don't have to be in the same room to be aware of each other.'

'You walked away from me after that night at the villa,' Emily reminded him shakily.

'Because you made me angry. Very angry. But I soon discovered that it didn't stop me from still wanting—needing—you.'

Needing—that was a new word; Emily had never heard him use it before, not of anything or anyone. She blinked hard, trying to clear her suddenly over-bright eyes. Then she forced herself to extinguish deliberately the small spark of hope that had ignited inside her.

'I don't think you mean that,' she said sadly at last. 'You're not a man who'll ever need anyone. You lead your own life, you're completely self-sufficient. You've got your work, your family—that's enough for you. You're not interested in anything else. You told me that yourself.'

'I lied,' Nikolaos said simply. 'To you, and to myself. I've always wanted more, but I wouldn't let myself have it. In the end, I convinced myself that I didn't even want it. I'd seen what love could do, the damage it could cause when it went wrong. I told myself that no one was ever going to get the chance to wreck my life like that. But now I find that I want to take that chance. I want to take it with you, Emily.'

She almost stopped breathing. But she still couldn't quite believe it.

'You should marry a Cypriot girl,' she said slowly. 'Someone who knows you and understands you. Someone like——' It was incredibly hard to get the last couple of words out. 'Someone like Sofia,' she finally finished in a painful tone.

Nikolaos gave her an unexpectedly rough shake. 'If I'd wanted to marry Sofia, I would have done it years ago. And you might not have been born here, but you belong here. As soon as you set foot on the island of love, you began to change. Your skin was turned to pale honey by the sun, your eyes brightened, your hair was so glossy and full of life that I wanted to touch it every time I saw it.' He suddenly laughed at the startled look on her face. 'You didn't know that, did you? Just how hard I had to fight to keep my hands off you? And I didn't always succeed, of course. I found excuses to kiss you. That lovely mouth,' he said more softly, running just one finger over the trembling outline of her lips, 'the colour of our sweetest wine. And then I made the mistake of taking you to the haunts of Aphrodite, and discovered that you already knew all her secrets——'

His voice was dark and husky now, and he was so close that just one small movement of her body would mean they would be touching.

'Stay here with me. Forever,' he invited thickly. 'If you get homesick, I'll take you back to England for a holiday. But only in the summer, so that you're always warm and honey-coloured. No more freezing English winters and pale faces. I don't want you ever again to be that cold little English girl that I first met in the solicitor's office.'

'I won't be,' she promised softly. 'And I do want to stay here for the rest of my life. With you.'

Nikolaos drew in a quick, unsteady breath. Then he bent his head and kissed her.

It was several minutes later before he raised his head again and gave a brilliant smile. By then, Emily felt as if her body was ready to melt away completely if he touched her just one more time. Her skin was on fire, every inch of her seemed to ache for him, and she could feel the hot urgency of love running through his own body.

'I hope that you're prepared for the full ritual of a Cypriot wedding,' he said, his hand already stroking her again, as if to caress away any protests she might be going to make. 'My aunts have been waiting for my marriage for years. They are going to insist on a huge affair, with probably half the island invited.'

'Everyone can come,' Emily said dazedly. 'I don't care.' Then her eyes suddenly focused clearly again for a few moments. 'You will invite Eléni, won't you?'

Nikolaos hesitated for only a fraction of a second. 'Yes,' he said in a firm voice.

Emily relaxed again. Then Nikolaos's fingers ran slowly down her spine and his voice murmured in her ear, 'We haven't discussed children.'

She looked at him slightly anxiously. 'You do want them, don't you?'

'Of course,' he said at once. 'The only question to be settled is — how many?'

'Oh, as many as you like,' Emily said generously.

Nikolaos grinned. 'This is very new, giving in so easily to whatever I ask of you. I think that I like it. What else shall I ask?'

'Anything,' she said softly, totally acquiescent in his arms.

'Do you still have your master key?'

'Yes,' Emily said, slightly surprised.

'Then I think that I shall ask you to lock the door,' Nikolaos said in a voice that had suddenly thickened again.

It took her only seconds to obey him. Then she was back in his arms again, and his hands were moving lovingly over her, gentle and yet urgent, swiftly unfastening clothes, seeking out the hot, eager body beneath. And the words of love they both whispered were sometimes in Greek and sometimes in English, but the language didn't matter — being together was the only thing of any importance.

The sun shone hotly through the window, the crystal-clear sea lapped gently against the shores of the island of love, and maybe Aphrodite herself smiled gently as she spun her old magic for a new pair of lovers.

CYPRUS — 'the island of love'

Cyprus is the birthplace of the goddess of love, Aphrodite, and, with its natural beauty, there could be no more fitting place for her. Past and present live side by side here, while the island glows with the love of life the Cypriots are known for. So come to the island that promises to offer you 'the warmest welcome in the Meditteranean'.

THE ROMANTIC PAST

Cyprus stands between three continents — Europe, Asia and Africa — and its colourful history is filled with battles and invasions. It was populated as far back as 5800BC, and has since been ruled by, among others, the Greeks, Egyptians, Romans and British.

Many famous names are associated with the history of Cyprus. The island fell into the hands of **Alexander the Great** in 331BC, and nearly three hundred years later it was given by **Antony** to **Cleopatra** as a symbol of his love for her.

In 1191 **Richard the Lion Heart** arrived in Cyprus. A previous ship carrying his sister and his fiancée, Berengaria, had already landed, and the cruel ruler of the time was about to attack the ship and carry them off by force. Richard was incensed that anyone should dare to insult his ladies in this way, and he defeated the leader and forced him to flee. Shortly afterwards Richard and Berengaria sealed their love by getting married in Limassol.

Aphrodite, the goddess of love and beauty, supposedly originated in Cyprus. She is said to have risen naked from the waves on a scallop-shell near Paphos. She was so beautiful that flowers grew at her feet wherever she walked, and she is renowned for her many lovers. However, lest anyone should cast aspersions at her morality, it is said that she returned to Paphos from time to time to renew her virginity in the sea!

However, the course of true love didn't always run smooth — even for the goddess of love herself! Aphrodite fell in love with **Adonis**, the symbol of beauty and love, but so did **Persephone**, the goddess of the underworld. The dispute was finally settled when **Zeus** declared that Adonis should spend half a year with each of them.

Cyprus is now split into two parts, with the Turks controlling about a third of the island, in the northern part of Cyprus, and the Greek Cypriots controlling the rest of the country.

here is still a delightful sense of living history in
yprus, with the many historic sites and quaint cus-
ms. Models of sick people, dedicated to the saints
ho may be able to cure them, can occasionally be
en in country churches, while if you come across
ndkerchiefs hanging from trees it probably means
at there is a shrine with magical properties near by.

HE ROMANTIC PRESENT — pastimes for lovers. . .

ne of the most attractive towns to base yourself in
ust be **Paphos**, on the south-west coast of the island.
'hen you first arrive, why not soak up the relaxed
mosphere by wandering along by the sea front and
lmiring the views of **Paphos Fortress** and the harbour?

ut while you're walking, don't be surprised if you
me across one of the more unusual residents of
iphos — one of the pelicans which can often be seen
andering around near the harbour!

you've come to Cyprus to rediscover romance, the
aths of Aphrodite, a short drive from Paphos, must be
e ideal place to start. In this quiet, peaceful spot is a
ool where Aphrodite is said to have bathed. She met
any of her lovers here, and those she rejected suppos-
lly walked to a nearby spring to cool their inflamed
assions in the cold water!

ut if, rather than rejecting your partner, you want to
icourage him to be *more* loving, perhaps you should
ove on to the nearby **Fontana Amorosa** (The Fountain
Love). According to legend, anyone who drinks the
ater from one of the wells here will fall in love!

Another site which has seen romance and passion f
centuries, is the **Temple of Aphrodite**, not far fro
Paphos. Here the sexual impulse was praised a
celebrated, and there were festivals and rites encou
aging fertility. Nowadays you can wander hand in ha
with your partner and imagine all the lovers who ha
been here before you.

Back in Paphos itself, there's an opportunity to live o
childhood dreams of being an explorer. Visit t
'Byzantine' fortress and see the intriguing ruins of wh
could once have been a Crusader castle. You can roa
around at will, descending crumbling staircases, disco
ering dead ends and unexpected corners — and th
coming face to face with your partner at the mo
unexpected junctions!

Visitors to Paphos shouldn't miss the **House**
Dionysus, a third-century Roman villa, where you
find a superb display of mosaic floors, mainly showi
mythological and hunting scenes.

And when the sun goes down and it's time to ea
adjourn to an intimate little taverna with dim lighti
and brightly coloured tablecloths. Order a *meze* — a
then sit back in amazement as dish after dish is broug
to your table. To begin with there will be dips such
homous (ground chick peas in oil and garlic) a
taramasalata, served with sesame-seed bread. Next y
will be brought fish and meat dishes such as *souvla*
(skewered pieces of lamb grilled over charcoal) a
stifado (a beef stew with wine, onions and herbs
When the dishes finally stop coming, only the bra
few will be able to manage a sweet dessert like *bakla*
(a strudel-like pastry with honey and nuts), but y

may well be able to find room for some delicious fresh fruit.

And to accompany your meal, what could be better than one of the wines Cyprus has been famous for since antiquity? Try **Commandaria**, a sweet dessert wine, if you want to discover what wine was like in medieval times. Or try the aniseed-flavoured aperitif called **uzo** — but take care, as it's quite strong!

After a few glasses of alcohol and with the holiday spirit filling you, you might well find yourself getting up from your table and joining in one of the spontaneous dances that often take place to the sound of **bouzouki** music towards the end of the evening! Eating out in Paphos is certainly an unforgettable experience!

While there's enough to keep you happy in Paphos for at least a week, Cyprus has so much to discover that it seems a shame not to venture further. The towns of **Larnaca**, **Nicosia** and **Limassol** all have much to offer, or for a change you can discover the quaint, sparsely populated little villages or get away from it all in the serenity of the **Troodos Mountains**.

Don't forget to leave time for looking for souvenirs before you go home, though! Try one of the Cyprus handicraft shops, where you can buy some world-famous **Lefkara lace**. Basket-making is another traditional craft, so why not take home a little cheese-basket — filled, of course, with a packet of the local **halloumi** cheese? It's the perfect memento to remind you of Cyprus's centuries-old traditions and wonderful cuisine at the same time!

DID YOU KNOW THAT. . .?

* Cyprus is the **third largest Mediterranean islan** after Sicily and Sardinia.

* There are one hundred and twenty varieties c **flowers** that grow nowhere else in the world excep Cyprus.

* Like the British, the Cypriots drive on the left-han side of the road.

* Because of its mild winters, Northern Europea athletes and football teams sometimes use Cyprus a their training ground.

* When they want to say 'I love you' the romanti Cypriots murmur, '*S'ayapō*.'

POSTCARDS FROM EUROPE

HARLEQUIN PRESENTS®

Travel across Europe in 1994 with Harlequin Presents. Collect a new Postcards From Europe title each month!

Don't miss
VIKING MAGIC
by Angela Wells
Harlequin Presents #1691

Available in October, wherever Harlequin Presents books are sold.

HPPFE10

Hi!
The last thing I expected—or needed— when I arrived in Copenhagen was a lecture. But that's what Rune Christensen proceeded to give me. He clearly blames me for the disappearance of my sister and _his_ nephew. If only Rune wasn't so attractive.

Love, Gina

Where do you find hot Texas nights, smooth Texas charm and dangerously sexy cowboys?

Crystal Creek reverberates with the exciting rhythm of Texas. Each story features the rugged individuals who live and love in the Lone Star state.

"...Crystal Creek wonderfully evokes the hot days and steamy nights of a small Texas community...impossible to put down until the last page is turned." —*Romantic Times*

Praise for Bethany Campbell's *The Thunder Rolls*

"Bethany Campbell takes the reader into the minds of her characters so surely...one of the best Crystal Creek books so far. It will be hard to top...." —*Rendezvous*

"This is the *best* of the Crystal Creek series to date." —*Affaire de Coeur*

Don't miss the next book in this exciting series. Look for **GENTLE ON MY MIND** by BETHANY CAMPBELL

Available in October wherever Harlequin books are sold.

CC-20

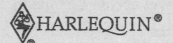

®HARLEQUIN®

Weddings, Inc.

THE VENGEFUL GROOM
Sara Wood

Legend has it that those married in Eternity's chapel are destined for a lifetime of happiness. But happiness isn't what Giovanni wants from marriage—it's revenge!

Ten years ago, Tina's testimony sent Gio to prison—for a crime he didn't commit. *Now* he's back in Eternity and looking for a bride. *Now* Tina is about to learn just how ruthless and disturbingly sensual Gio's brand of vengeance can be.

THE VENGEFUL GROOM, available in October from Harlequin Presents, is the fifth book in Harlequin's new cross-line series, **WEDDINGS, INC.** Be sure to look for the sixth book, **EDGE OF ETERNITY,** by Jasmine Cresswell (Harlequin Intrigue #298), coming in November.

Travel across Europe in 1994
with Harlequin Presents and...

As you travel across Europe in 1994, visiting your favorite countries with your favorite authors, don't forget to collect four proofs of purchase to redeem for an appealing photo album. This photo album can hold over fifty 4"×6" pictures of your travels and will be a precious keepsake in the years to come!

One proof of purchase can be found in the back pages of each POSTCARDS FROM EUROPE title...one every month until December 1994.

To receive your gift, please fill out the information below and mail four (4) original proof-of-purchase coupons from any Harlequin Presents POSTCARDS FROM EUROPE title plus $3.00 for postage and handling (check or money order—do not send cash), payable to Harlequin Books, to: IN THE U.S.: P.O. Box 9048, Buffalo, NY, 14269-9048; IN CANADA: P.O. Box 623, Fort Erie, Ontario, L2A 5X3.

Requests must be received by January 31, 1995.
Please allow 4–6 weeks after receipt of order for delivery.

Name: _____
Address: _____
_____
City: _____
State/Province: _____
Zip/Postal Code: _____
Account No: _____
ONE PROOF OF PURCHASE

077 KBY